Tales from the Heart.

A Collection of New Writing from Athlone Institute of Technology.

First published March 2019.
Edited by Mick Donnellan.
www.mickdonnellan.com

Special thanks to the staff at AIT and especially those in the Department of LifeLong Learning. This publication would not have been possible without their invaluable support. Particular thanks are due to Michael Tobin, Seadna Ryan, Maria Slevin, Janine King, Jenny Burke and John Carroll.

Contributors:

1. **David Flynn** - *Interview with Maeve Binchy*

2. **David Whelan** - *Strength*

3. **Aideen O'Hara** - *The Unlocked Door, The Journey, Psyche Ward*

4. **Anne Mare Crehan** - *No Need for a key + The Stations*

5. **John McLoughlin** - *1461 Days + Stepping Up*

6. **Peggy Garvey** - *Winter + Moving House*

7. **Joe Dowling** - *A Rough Form of Justice, April, The Ballykeeran Oak*

8. **Janice Dobbie** - *Her Birthday + Big Brother*

9. **Ray O'Brien** - *Death of a Future.*

10. **Oliver Higgins** - *Never Too Late to Educate + In Search of a Ghost*

11. **Marva Fitzpatrick** - *Harold's Letter*

12. **Chantalle Loughran** - *The Ghostbusters + Alice*

13. **Caroline Coyle (Guest Speaker)** - *My daddy didn't hold me down*

14. **Jennifer McCarthy** - *The Devil's Pirouette*

15. **Olivia Caffrey** - *Home*

16. **Bernie Doyle** - *The Precious Present*

17. **Sheila Mahon** - *Leaving Legacy*

18. **Gina Dunne** - *The Gathering*

Foreword

Writing is not easy. You make sacrifices. You give up time with your family and friends. You miss special occasions. You lose concentration in the middle of conversations because you're thinking about a story. You dream of breaking through one day. Getting a book accepted, a Play produced, a film made, your article in the paper. It can often feel like a vague concept - something on the far side of that which you intend to create. But how can you create it? You don't know any other writers. You don't know anything about publishing. You have bills to pay. A family to feed. Pressure from your day job. But all the while is that candle burning in the back of your mind, urging you to say what you want to say, get your message out there. Be heard. So you take the first step and join a writing class. Suddenly you are surrounded by like-minded people. You don't feel like a social outcast anymore. Here are other artists that read the books you read, write the Poetry you like, watch the same films and even like to go to the theatre. It's a new world. One with guidance and direction and access to advice. You feel secure sharing your work. You get constructive feedback. Writing hacks that can help you get through your day. You develop techniques to find inspiration, a sense of structure and something to work towards. Next week it's Short Stories, last week it was Fiction. Tonight we're looking at Screenwriting. This is brilliant. But then the class ends and what now? What did we achieve? We know how to write, what to write about, the best times and places to do it, but what about the end goal: Getting published. Getting those stories out there. Getting heard. And that's where this publication comes in.

Some of the writers have been taking the course since it began - eighteen months ago. Others just started in January. But the question always hung the air: How do we get to the next step? Apply what we've learned? How do we see our work in print? Thing being, getting published is traditionally difficult. The best of of writers often only breakthrough after years of trying and literally hundreds of rejections. Even better writers never get recognised at all. So we decided to put this collection together. Not to wait and leave our creative dreams to the fate of an uncaring world.

I knew the quality in the class was outstanding and deserved to be published. Each student committed to having something ready. Something that would reflect their talent and highlight their creative spirit. Every story here is told from the heart. Each poem is measured and profound. I'm always astounded by the wealth of experience each of these writers bring to the page. Every contribution displays an uncanny understanding of the human soul and weaves a tale with great depth and artistic dexterity. And most of all, it gives each creator the magic experience of turning their work from lead to gold. A writer can spend years with his or her best work left lost in a shoebox or buried in a hard drive somewhere. But it takes an opportunity like this to bring it to fruition and give it life. It helps a writer actualise - to become the artist they are destined to be - armed with the knowledge that it is immensely possible.

Today is also a day that is unique for every contributor here. Because there are days when you go through the motions. You go to work, you deal with life, you take what comes but you don't truly feel like you are on the right path. You are not fulfilled. You are not satisfied. And then there are days when you get published. When you get to say what you want to say. You wake up and the world around you has a different quality to it. You are stepping into the future you have dreamed of, past the imaginary barriers that have kept you inhibited. You have overcome the anxiety and worry about whether or not you are capable. You have done what hundreds of writers only dream of every day - you have been published. Your work has become gold and now there are no limits.

Mick Donnellan.

Maeve Binchy - A bookish and exciting life

By

David Flynn

I interviewed best-selling author Maeve Binchy at her home in Dalkey, Co. Dublin in November 2010. She was always a reader, not necessarily always a writer, but she has lived a life which has beaten any of the excitements she found in the likes of Gone With The Wind and other such books.

"Our house in Dalkey was always filled with books, and my father used to always buy a paperback book to read on the train, rather than a newspaper," *said Maeve Binchy, in an interview with this writer.* "The whole family would sit and read in the home and in the garden, and I loved fiction, rather than biographies, because I'm not interested in real lives."

Maeve was one of four children, and always refused to write an autobiography and she believed that she shouldn't allow intrusion into her sibling's lives, and that people would only want to know about her if they lived through alcoholism or poverty. However she says everything was the opposite, and was a real happy childhood.

"We lived in a loving home, and some would call it smug, but we were lucky, and I'm very grateful for that and there are no deep dark secrets in there," she laughed. "I'm always cheerful about things, and attitude is very important, because here I am at 70 years of age, and I'm fat, but I don't say: "Oh poor me!" I just think it's fantastic that I'm still here, with enough money to build a lift in my house, because I can't get upstairs very well."

Maeve Binchy's bestselling novels are mostly set in Ireland, or with an Irish background. No matter where in the world a booklover searches a bookshop, they would likely see one or more Binchy novels adorning the shop's bookshelves. She lives in Dalkey, Co. Dublin not far from where she grew up. Among her most famous titles, are 'Light a Penny Candle', 'Circle of Friends', 'Evening Class', 'Scarlett Feather', and the book which shot her to international fame, 'Tara Road'. Chat show host, Oprah Winfrey built an episode of her hit television series around Maeve and 'Tara Road' in 2000.

"A few years before that, US first lady, Barbara Bush had mentioned me during an interview with Oprah, and that made me take off in America, but then I was invited to the programme to discuss 'Tara Road', which Oprah had put into her book club slot," said Maeve.

Maeve does agree that she is a happy person, and one who looks on life as the glass being half full.

"My parents thought all their children were the bees' knees and that we were all great," said Maeve.

Maeve went to convent school, and then to UCD to do a degree, and after graduating in 1963, she went to Israel to work in a kibbutz, a collective community where she picked fruit from morning till night, and experienced a new life journey. She wrote colourful letters home to her parents about her time in the kibbutz, and while she had no intention of being a writer, she intended to be a judge. She also lived in Greece for many summers, and in a US summer camp in New Hampshire.

"I was going to be a judge, not a barrister mind, but a judge. And my father was a barrister, and he spoke in awe of judges," she said. "Mothers didn't go out to work in those years of the 1940's, but stayed at home to mind us, and she was a nurse, and she could have been a great part-time nurse, but in those days, it would be said that a man couldn't keep his wife, if she went out to work, but we would have missed her, and it was the custom of the time."

Maeve's parents died while young, and it was a great shock to her and her siblings.

"When I came home from Israel, my father told me that the Irish press were publishing my letters to the family, and they did a big page entitled, 'Irish girl goes to Kibbutz,' and then I got a cheque for €17, which was more than a week's salary," said Maeve. "I thought it was very easy to be a writer, and had about ten articles accepted."

After she had become a secondary school teacher, Maeve did a series for the Irish Times about how she believed teachers understood fifteen year old girls better than their parents.

"Parents only see untidy rooms, but we see kids who want to cure famine and who write poetry," she said. "So that's what I did, I wrote about what I knew and cared about, and I'm still doing that, almost a half century later."

Maeve writes like she talks, and by her own admission she likes to talk her own way and not with a fancy accent. She has a great memory and remembers everything about her childhood growing up in Dalkey, and she remembers little things like tins of broken biscuits, and red fizzy lemonade that went up her nose when she drank it with a straw.

Maeve loves writing her novels and short stories, and publishers nervously ring her up some time after her latest book, and ask her if has she an idea for a new book.

"You put your idea on one page, and if you can't put it on one page, it's not going to sell," said Maeve. "Otherwise you can go on and on endlessly."

She likes books by Fay Weldon, a writer who she met several times over the past few years. She also liked reading 'Gone with the Wind', and Daphne Du Maurier's 'Frenchman's Creek' and 'Jamaica Inn.' She plays "desperately bad bridge, with a glass of chardonnay," as she says herself, and plays chess with her 93 old neighbour.

"He makes a chess move through the cat flap in our door everyday, and he's a lovely man," she said.

In the 1970's, Maeve met the love of her life, children's book author, Gordon Snell, while she worked on BBC Radio 4's Woman's Hour, and while Gordon worked for BBC Overseas Service. They became friends for a few years, and didn't fall in love straight away, but married almost 35 years ago.

Maeve loves working in her office, which fits comfortably into the attic of her Dalkey home. Maeve and Gordon sit side by side writing their different style of books on two laptops.

"I love working in this room, and ideally we get up in the morning, and have breakfast around 8.30 am, which is usually porridge and croissants, and then we come up here around 9.30 am, and work till around 1pm," said Maeve from the comfort of her attic office.

She has worked in the office through ill health as much as possible and generally writes 2,000 words per day, but the most surprising thing of all that she reveals is that she has written 16 bestselling novels, with not a shred of research.

"I do no research, and I only write about things that don't have to have research, but with my latest novel, 'Minding Frankie', I did need to research two things," she said. "I had to research DNA, so I rang of friend of mine who works in that kind of stuff, and I needed to know when would the

Catholic Church assume that a missing person was dead, and I rang a priest friend of mine, who said that it depends on each case."

The idea for 'Minding Frankie', which is another No. 1 book for Maeve Binchy, came while she was passing a school one day, and saw many people waiting outside for children to come out, and there were many mothers, grannies and brothers collecting children.

"Families have completely changed so much from when I was young, and there are now many one parent families, and I imagined a story where one recovering alcoholic man is the single parent of a baby," said Maeve. "He goes to Alcoholics Anonymous, and he is trying to be a good father, but the odds are stacked against him. I'm very happy with the way the story worked out, and there are lots of ups and downs in it for the characters."

Some of her bestselling novels have been made into movies, most notably, 'Circle of Friends' starring Chris O'Donnell and Minnie Driver and 'Tara Road', which starred Andie McDowell.

"I never get involved in the screenplays of my books so I just let the film companies get on with it, and there was a lot of publicity a few years back about one of my books, 'Evening Class' being optioned by 20th Century Fox, but then they lost interest," said Maeve. "I will listen to people if they say the book is wrong, and I've a good editor in America, who discovered Tracy Chevalier, Harlen Coben, Danielle Steele and Nicholas Evans, and she found all of these people just from manuscripts, and I trust her completely."

Maeve is with her agent, Christine, from when she wrote her first bestseller, 'Light A Penny Candle' in 1982. 'Circle of Friends' is loosely based on Maeve's own life, and she says she is a bit like the female heroine, Benny.

"Benny is a bit like me, but I didn't have the life she has, and I was vulnerable and made an eejit of myself," she laughed. "I don't like perfect characters, and when I read a book, I like ordinary characters. I don't like makeover stories, but what the people do get in my stories, is characters that develop confidence, because if you have confidence you can do anything."

Maeve thinks she'll write another novel in the near future, and while she believed she'd retire just over a decade ago, she was talked out of retirement.

"I thought I was too old, and was getting tired, and I wasn't able to be travelling eleven days in America and then six days in the North of England," she said.

Maeve and Gordon are very happy living their Dalkey lives in the company of creatures great and small.

"We are very lucky, but we didn't have children, and we were too old when we realised that, to adopt, but we borrowed everybody else's children," said Maeve. "I have two gorgeous cats, Fred and Dorothy, and Dorothy has not been blessed with brains and thinks her tail is another animal following her."

Maeve said she couldn't be like Gordon and write a children's book because she was a teacher many years ago, and would feel like she should be trying to improve children. Also she unashamedly tells adults through her books, to not be self-conscious and to get over themselves.

"Life as a writer is great nowadays, because all you have to do is press a button and send something to 46 countries, and it's not like years ago, when the telephone was in the cold hall, and everyone in the family could hear your conversation when you were ringing some fellow, and your mother would then ask you who it is," said Maeve laughing.

Maeve believes she is lucky in life, because she has everything she has wanted – except children. She bought her house in Dalkey in 1980, and it helped that 'Light a Penny Candle' was a huge success in the early 80's, which helped her build up her house.

"I've always been an optimist, even when I had nothing," she said.

Sadly, Maeve died in July 2012.

Strength

By

David Whelan

What's the difference between having strength and being strong? The question circles endlessly in my head as I wash the blood from my face, dry brown flakes falling like snow onto the white porcelain, lingering briefly before being caught in the current, vanishing down the plughole. Just because you have strength does that make you strong? No, that isn't right, the boys at lunch everyday are not strong. Individually I could probably fight them off. Kick them. Punch them. Bloody their noses. But they never show up one by one. It's always in a group. That's where their strength comes from. I think of the latest time, as I dry my face, red on white, tossing the towel into the bin as I make my way into the kitchen.

Late in the lunch period, Mr Davis sneaking off duty early to do a line as usual, they came for me. Five in all, they approached me from every angle, reaching out to grab me. I tried to evade, slip through, but there was no way out. Together they managed to pin me down, their strength in numbers making them strong enough to hold me in place. Nobody came to help me. Nobody ever did. Some people did look up though, eager, ready for their weekly dinner time show. That was when he arrived.

Ronan Turing. He's the fat kid in class. Just 5 Feet tall, and at nearly 200 pounds, you'd expect him to be the target of mockery. Instead he is their leader, venomous words twisting their minds, turning the focus of that pent up aggression and hormonal hatred to a new target: Me.

I've never figured out how they singled me out. I was always quiet, unobtrusive, blending into the background of the school scene. Perhaps, I now wonder, if that is exactly why they did, my silence somehow offending them.

And so each day they come for me. Pin me down. Make me a sacrifice to their lord, offering it up in the hopes of elevating their own status in the schools sordid hierarchy. Ronan is strong, his bulk crushing as he straddles my prone form, neck cracking as he rolls his shoulders, loosening them. His weight makes him strong, but he has no strength in his punches. He has to hit me quite a few times to draw blood, or maybe he just likes to prolong each of these sessions. He may have had no strength initially, but each beat down he rendered unto me *gave it to him*. His blows like fangs, tearing into my being, sapping my strength to augment his own as he sits atop me, growing fat on it like an overgrown leech. His audience at the canteen tables nod and chuckle to themselves, sealing the transfer of power, ensuring what has been stolen can never return to me.

I move gingerly from the bathroom downstairs into the kitchen, both because the bruises on my ribs are making themselves known, and I didn't want to wake the beast slumbering on the couch in the living room. Moving carefully, I shuffle across the yellowed linoleum floor towards the fridge. Opening the door slowly, the light is gone again, not that there was much in here to shine on, I began to pick the dirty ice cubes out of the ice box, one by one, placing them onto a mouldering tea towel. The ice suddenly crackles, settling, and I pause, ears straining. The beast snorts and shuffles a bit, but keeps sleeping. Relieved, I catch the corners of the tea towel and bring them together, lifting me shirt to press it against my ribs, relishing the chill that sweeps over my chest.

As I make my way back across the floor, my intent is to spend the remaining hours of the day nursing my wounds in preparation for tomorrow's event. Suddenly, I pause. For some reason I can't explain I turn and creep towards the other door, half ajar, the one leading to the living room, the residence of the sleeping beast. Peeking around the corner he comes into view, unconscious upon his throne, its pleather faded and worn, studded with a myriad of cigarette burns. Empty bottles make a minefield of the floor, a misstep liable to draw more of my blood before the day's end. I turn my gaze from the detritus of his hoard back to observing the beast, the man, my father. He's shorter than me, grizzled unkempt beard yellowing and nicotine stained, a stocky frame that was strong in his prime but it's long since gone to seed, never to sprout again. In its place weeds have sprung up, choking and hateful, which he waters with cheap booze. Occasionally they bear fruit, bursting explosively into a rage that drives him from this room, his room, in search of a place to spread its seeds. Since mum left, he's inevitably lead to my room. Beatings soften the soil of my soul, his vitriolic seeds burrowing deep into the tilled soil, spreading poison. I sometimes wonder if the others in my class experience this too, their efforts to destroy me evidence of the dark flowers blooming within their own souls. But no, if it were true then they'd just kill me rather then toy with me as they do each day. It's what I would do.

I'm still unsure as to why I came in here to look at him. Perhaps it was just to make sure he was truly out of it and not just faking as he's done before. The stain around his crotch tells me he really is comatose this time. I close the door carefully and make my way back upstairs. The ice has begun to melt, the water trickling down to wet my pants, my only good pair. I make it into my bedroom and close the door behind me, putting the ice pack down to move my chair, my only piece of furniture, up under the door handle in case he wakes in the night.

As I undress I toss my belt onto the bed, glancing at it and thinking back to all the times my father has turned it on me. Like with Ronan, there's no strength in him, rather it's the weapons he wields, like the belt, that give him strength. That make him strong. That's it, isn't it? Being strong doesn't necessarily mean you have strength, but having strength of some kind will make you strong, and that strength can come from many things. The number of people with you, the way you outwardly display yourself, the way the other person sees you. Objects. Objects can give you strength. Objects can make you strong. *Objects can make you strong.* The phrase is going off in my head like a firecracker, this sudden epiphany taking my breath away. Even if nobody else in school would take my side, giving me the strength of their back against mine. Even if nobody would believe me when I spoke out against this daily ritual, Ronan's honeyed words deafening sympathetic ears. Even if I couldn't make others treat me with respect, too much of my standing had already been siphoned out. Despite all these things I could still do something.

Taking the chair away from my door I unlock it and stride back into the hall, suddenly uncaring of the noise I am making. I make my way straight into what was my parent's room. A quick search and I find it, hidden poorly by some shoes and a box of old photos, my parents wedding. The box is a small plain thing, walnut with a simple latch. I undo it, the lid springs open, and I reach for what's inside. The grip is cold, the stippled stock rough yet somehow comforting in my hand. Two other smaller boxes lie within as well, clattering when I shake them, telling me I have more than what I'd need. As I hold it I can feel something rising within me, something I'd almost forgotten. Strength. It's like boiling oil in my veins, exploding into my heart and melting my brain. Strength. With this in my hand giving me strength I am strong. Strong enough to do the things I couldn't before. Tomorrow I will prove that to those in school. And they will see how strong I am.

    Briefly.

The Unlocked Door

By

Aideen O'Hara

Benny kicked stones with his well-scuffed boots and swaggered his way down the suburban street. Barnes, the school principal, was jaded by his truancy. He was never going to pass his SATS, despite his Mom's tireless appeals. School sucked. Life sucked. He needed to make a few bucks, then slide off to the pool hall in Park Lane, knock back a beer, smoke a joint or two, get laid.

Shiftily, he glanced around him. All was still. The octogenarians who lived here were usually gone on a Friday, collecting benefits, meeting for tea. With a sharp eye out for trouble, he sidled into each back yard, tried the door, then strolled back to the street again. Those shambling old timers often forgot to close up properly. They often kept savings hidden in a drawer. Banks were the last place they trusted. Sometimes Benny got lucky. He needed luck today

He was working his way smartly along the strip. The next house was gloomy, all greys and duns, with wild mushrooms sprouting thickly beneath the gutter. One of the downstairs shutters was loose, and it rapped against the peeling plasterwork, relentlessly. Creepy, thought Benny, but he never missed a house. Glancing about him, he sidled round to the backdoor, noting the large galvanised shed and the thicket of trees behind it. All was still.

His gloved hand tried the door and the handle gave way smoothly, inviting him in. The door opened to a cold concrete room within. All was silent, save for the whirring hum of a deep freeze, pushed right to the back wall, white in the gloom and clean in the squalor.

Transfixed, he moved towards it. A sure spot for a hoard of dollars. He cranked the lid open. A white fog rose to freeze him. Waving it away, he peered in. Peered far in and saw what he'd rather not see – a mass, a large one, a stooge, dead as diamonds, its face leering upwards, black teeth, stubble, a deadly grimace. He opened his mouth in a silent scream, frozen as the freezer creature.

Suddenly, a noise out back, a door banging closed. Squeaky steps in the distance. Nowhere to hide but the icy grave before him. Heavy steps approaching, dragging a load. He climbed inside, a trickle of urine landing on the Stiff, freezing instantly.

The door banged open. A heavy tread matched up to a dragging sound as the homeowner pulled a leaden weight across the floor. Benny couldn't feel his fingers. His bladder leaked some more. Then a thud, as the bulky weight hit the freezer.

Benny flatlined, then filled with frenzy. With a tribal cry, he shot from his deathbed, hair wiry with frost and eyes like coals from deepest Hades. The Stiff had a shovel buried with him. The frost burned Benny's hands as he gripped it. He swung, then ran.

That was Benny in the olden days. Now he's a cop, living in Vermont, dealing in Stiffs, but none like the first Stiff, the brother of the guy he whacked. That guy was working his way through his family.

The Journey

She sat in the dark taxi, heart thumping,
And watched the lights glide by.
Ten euro for a five minute walk.
But then it was Dublin, a bad area, and dark.
She'd come with a suitcase and plastic bags
Bulging with blankets.
Hurriedly packed,
Desperate to leave.
Panicked, in case they'd stop her,
Like before.
In case she'd never escape.

Heuston loomed.
The taxi man was kind.
He knew where she'd come from.
She drove the trolley he'd loaded through to the barrier.
Her ticket was void, a cardboard receipt, the other back where she'd bought it.
She cried, and told them where she'd been.
Full of care and kindness, they let her on,
Determined, dragging her mountain of bags.
She wept the long way home.
Desperate suffering behind her
And desperate suffering to come.

Aideen O'Hara.

Psyche Ward

By

Aideen O'Hara

They've thrown her into solitary, injecting her first so she could not resist. She lies on the floor and comes to in a haze. Remembers the strong legs scuffling, big men pinning her down. She'd screamed for Catherine. Catherine had stood by, shocked and watchful, unable to reply.

She turns on her back now, with a groan. Contemplates screaming, but the place is padded. They can't hear a thing. One small square lights the compartment. It's white and murky outside. She starts to fidget, has nothing to do. Her mind races, remembers.

They brought her here for a Paid Holiday, one she didn't want but had to take. Emphasising the necessity, the wardens clamped her down and carried her to her room. Her cries were laced with horror, terror-struck. Later she met the other inmates, together suspended in a strange new reality, made embryonic by the mandates and sanctions of the place. Only she and Catherine railed against it, bombarding the desk staff with anger and ire. And together they scouted the enclosed garden, watched over, searching for a way of escape.

Today is her birthday. Nobody knows. A spider walks delicately up the cell wall, drawn by the small square of brightness high up near the ceiling, too far for her to reach.

She's churned up, her mind humming. The tiled floor glows where the diamonds intersect. If she concentrates, colours bounce up from the corners, playing a silent symphony.

The spider swings down gradually on a strand he's made. He seems impervious to the dancing colours, ploughing through the glowing field.

When she was young, she was innocent. A baby, delighting in a swinging mobile, watching her fat hands wave. She loved her gurgle, her chuckle, her scream. She didn't ask for abduction, degradation, a trauma so enormous it crippled her control.

Nobody asks to live a long life of hellish terror. Terror of the ailment, of the treatment, capture and disdain. And a fear for her privacy, that she would be outed, uncovered, unmasked. And a longing for a soulmate, but no soulmate wants such a crucible, such a trial.

She watches the fat spider for a moment. Industrious being, content in himself.

The door creaks. She recognises the jailer as one of her assailants – huge, burly, pitiless, his vast bulk useful in a place like this. He tries to grab her arm but she eludes him. Runs through the door, calling.

Catherine meets her, holds her, quiets her. Guides her to the window. Pure snowdrops drooping gracefully. A birthday greeting in a plastic mug, marked 'Hospital Property'.

Hospital Property, just like them.

The Stations

By

Anne Marie Crehan

'I think that's us father,' I say. I'm in my next door neighbour's house where our local priest has just said mass and asks the usual question: 'Who's taking the next station?'

While I say *I think* it means *I know* it's us because I have ascertained this well in advance of this evening. The stations generally follow a particular route so I have consulted with the station experts who are well versed in whether the stations are going out the road to Keogh's or down to Butler's. Anyway, it's settled, and the next station will be at our house next February. It's not compulsory to have the stations but it is a tradition that has existed for many, many years where I live and there is a fairly strong commitment to keep it going.

The stations are a very old custom where people take turns to have mass in their home. A parish is divided up into station areas, so it really is a local event and the mass is celebrated for close neighbours, family and friends.

The stations are steeped in tradition, dating back to the penal times when it was forbidden for catholic priests to say mass in public. In order to overcome this difficulty people took turns in having mass said in their homes. Word would spread quietly, and neighbours would gather to avail of the opportunity to hear mass. It was also against the law for priests to carry vestments or vessels used in the mass so the "mass kit" as it was known was passed on from house to house as it was needed, and the station mass as we now know it evolved from this. Even in these early days having the station involved a certain amount of preparation and this often included a collection that was used to ensure that another mass could be held.

Following the repeal of the penal laws the tradition of the station mass continued, mainly in rural areas and while it is now a much more relaxed affair the tradition of "getting ready" is still very strong.

Many householders, mainly women with myself included, saw the station as a glorious opportunity to tackle a multitude of jobs that had been left on the long finger. So, kitchens and sitting rooms were painted, curtains hung and worn out carpets and furniture replaced. In my own time, I quickly discovered that having the station had many advantages when looking for a tradesman. On moving into our new house over twenty years ago, gas fires were very much in vogue. The piping was put in place, the fire itself was purchased and my husband and I looked forward to toasting our toes on long winter nights. The plumber was supposed to come back to fit it. *Supposed to* …. he is a very busy man so alas, we were left to only *imagine* flickering flames for a few years until our turn to have the stations arrived. The plumber was duly contacted again, informing him of the upcoming event, and was there any chance of him being free? Well, it seems that the Lord himself has a lot of sway when it comes to plumbers because our hearth was glowing, warm and welcoming on the night. When I copped on to this leverage, I must admit that we may have had one or two more stations than were actually due but the new lights in the hall are gorgeous and the units in the sitting room are serving their purpose. So, while some people have found themselves under a bit of pressure with the preparations, I thank God for the stations and maybe some day I will confess my pretence to the carpenter and plumber.

The format of the stations has changed a lot over the years. Up until the late sixties the mass was always held in the mornings followed by breakfast that consisted of boiled eggs and homemade soda bread. An additional preparation for a morning station was that outside also had to be made presentable. Having a station in the morning involved the hosts getting up early putting on fires, filling kettles and pots to make tea and boil the eggs for the priest and visiting neighbours. Confessions were usually heard *before* mass, but this does not happen so much now. In the past fifty years, the option of having an evening station has come about, perhaps to accommodate people working outside of the home.

The tradition of providing refreshments after the mass continues to this day but the extent of the hospitality varies from house to house and parish to parish. Since the advent of having stations in the evenings, sandwiches, cakes with tea and coffee are regularly on the menu. However up until about twenty years ago it was not uncommon for the station host to serve a cold meat salad followed by an elaborate variety of sweet treats such as pavlova, apple tart, homemade Swiss Rolls and cakes. The station was an opportunity to showcase the domestic prowess of the host and "bought cake" was a non-runner! This was tricky if the woman of the house was shy in baking skills as competition was often very stiff. In recent times however, parish priests generally suggest that the catering should remain simple in an effort to keep the tradition of the stations alive and stress free. But whatever the fare on the table, no station was complete without a drop of the cratur or stout. Indeed, this made many a morning station linger long into the day.

Even children were not excluded from the gathering and were invited into the station house for something to eat on the way home from school.

My first experience of the station was that of a child growing up in east Galway. My siblings and I always enjoyed the excitement of the preparations especially when we were too young to be involved in any of the work. Indeed, we were probably in the way and I remember having to go to bed early when a bit of late evening painting was in progress. Our mother, a constant producer of home baked delights pulled out all the stops and treats that were usually reserved for Christmas appeared. A fire was put on early in the good room, again, used only at Christmas and for that night the usual MiWadi orange was put to the back of the press while we gassed up on fizzy orange and lemonade. Visiting neighbours kindly asked us about school, the work on the house was admired and the spread on the table appreciated.

At my first stations as the new Mrs. Crehan, the pressure was on.

'What will you give them?' My mother-in-law enquired. 'Sure you won't do *sandwiches*?'

It seemed an innocent enough query but the answer was in the question. 'You know you'll have a crowd? She said. 'First Station and all that.'

My own mother was also anxious that all would go well and was at hand to help, insisting that I say the apple tarts were all my own. With our first station we started a few new traditions. My mother-in-law gave us the loan of her crucifix with a fresh polish of Brasso and a bowl for holy water that belonged to her mother. This was to become our ritual each time we had the stations. I used my only white table cloth (a wedding present) and sure enough we had a crowd. The priest at the time was a man who liked to talk, it didn't matter if anyone wanted to listen, he was going to talk. He ended up with a lot to say that night as he was well fuelled with pioneer measures of some sort of brandy that my in-laws brought back from a recent visit to Medjugorie (there should be a health warning attached to leaving pioneers in charge of serving spirits). However, I was happy enough that everything went off without a hitch and our first station could be considered a success.

Since that night over twenty years ago the menu of cold meat salad has been dispensed with and to his credit, our now parish priest is a tea and a biscuit kind of man and does not expect people to feel under any pressure. We are obviously very good living people in our area as confessions rarely feature any more.

I still use the stations as motivation to do a few jobs around the house, don't look a gift horse in the mouth and all that! My husband and children, like the tradesmen, rally around with little resistance until the to-do list is completed. However, I find that I am less worried about the aesthetics and more looking forward to welcoming my now friends and not just neighbours into my home. The old saying: *If we hadn't the station, we would get nothing done!* Has been replaced by: *Were it not for the stations, when would we see each other?*

So, it's our turn next again. The cleaning will still be done and some outstanding jobs will be addressed. We will have some debate about what to have by way of food and absolutely some drinks will be purchased. The white tablecloth will make its usual appearance, fresh flowers and an altar arranged. By now *I am* making *my own* apple tarts! I am looking forward to catching up with everyone, remembering stations past. There are some people missing for various reasons. Older family members and neighbours who were stalwart station goers are no longer with us and while they may be physically absent, they will be remembered in conversations during the evening. Younger members of our community are in college or working away from home. Some have even emigrated, including our own daughter, who will be brought up to speed on all the news via Skype. I will have to polish my mother-in-law's crucifix myself this time as she needs a little more help with life now. Hopefully it will be up to the standard of previous years. The mass will be celebrated for all the people present and their intentions no matter how big or small. We will give thanks for the blessing of family, friends and neighbours. At the end the mass, Father will say: 'I wish God's blessing for health and happiness for each and every one of you.'

And I will say: 'Amen.'

No Need for a Key

By
Anne Marie Crehan

Aoife pushed down hard on the heavy door handle of her grandmother's old farmhouse and let herself into the dimly lit hallway that ran on to the kitchen.

'Hi, Granny. It's only me. Aoife.'

She inhaled the familiar smells of wood burning in the old stove and the faint scent of morning baking. White soda bread or maybe scones, you could always be sure of one or the other in granny's house. Not for the first time in her life did Aoife look forward to a cup of strong tea and whatever granny had taken from the oven earlier. And butter. *Real* butter.

Aoife was glad that her mother had been wrong about the door. Mum had told her to bring a key as the door could be locked, especially if granny was having a lie down.

'Locked?' Aoife was incredulous. 'That door is never locked.'

She smiled to herself with some satisfaction when she found it unlocked just as it had always been she was growing up.

Her grandmother's face broke into a warm smile when she laid eyes on her eldest granddaughter.

'How are you, love? This is a surprise. We don't usually see you on a Wednesday.'

'I have a few days off, so I thought I would pop home and say hello. Is everything alright granny? Just that mum said your door might be locked, what's that about, are you afraid granny?'

'Indeed, I'm not but we have the Community Alert here now and they are always calling, advising me. I don't like to offend them. They mean well so I turn the key now and again to keep them quiet. Put on the kettle there like a good girl. I made a few scones earlier.'

This was granny and granny's house at its best. Just the way Aoife loved it. She was glad that the door had been unlocked. It had been that way all her life since she was a small child, clambering through the gap in the hedge that was the boundary between Aoife's house and granny's. In the early days Aoife had her grandparents all to herself until the arrival of Michael when she was five. And while her grandfather passed away all too soon, granny was always there. A self-reliant, industrious woman, who reared turkeys and geese for the Christmas market right up until a few years ago. Now in her early eighties she was satisfied with keeping a few hens and the neighbours children often came round, all dying to help collect the eggs.

That unlocked door was an integral part of Aoife's life. Many an evening she flew through that door to proudly show granny the star she got from the teacher for her homework. She went through that door when she was sick and Mum had to go to work. Through that door, granny had doled out comfort and advice when she had her heart broken and when Aoife finally brought home her now husband and granny had given the seal of approval.

And Aoife had witnessed many changes to her *own* home since she was a child. Dad had finally gotten around to making the patio area that her mother had always wanted. Mum had changed her old bedroom into a guest room and yet her grandmother's house had remained relatively unchanged. She had so many wonderful memories of that house and it's unlocked door.

Cherished memories that she would love to share perhaps someday with her own children.

Aoife loved this house, it had always been important to her and at this moment it was more important than ever, now that granny was going to be a great grandmother.

1461 Days

By

John McLoughlin

The heat of the sun warmed the back of my neck as I stood there motionless. I was in a pensive mood, pleased with how well the flowers looked, slightly distracted by the somehow disrespectful chatter of the crows as they went about building their nests in some nearby trees. As always happens when I visit here, my mind drifted back to a day almost four years ago. Soon I was replaying a scene in my mind which I had replayed thousands of times before.

We were in the Sticky Pudding Café, just around the corner from my business, O'Shea's Garage, main dealers for Ford cars and tractors for over forty years. It was a Saturday afternoon and I had just finished work. It had been our custom at O'Shea's since my father started the business in 1965 to only open until lunchtime on Saturdays. Ruth, my partner, the love of my life, and our four year old daughter Lisa, the light of both our lives, had come into town to meet me after work.

Lisa had a milk brown moustache from the hot chocolate drink she had been dreaming about since last Saturday, and she was up to her elbows in a big chocolate muffin. Ruth and I sipped our Skinny Lattes and an Americanos as we planned a summer holiday in the south of France. As we talked excitedly we were oblivious to the comings and goings of other customers. Then, to our surprise, a plate of cookies and a cappuccino were laid in front of us on the table, and a large slightly scruffy man pulled a stool up beside me and sat down.

'Shea, you look like a million dollars,' was the greeting. It took me about a second to realise the man beside me was my old school buddy from our days in the CBS. He had never used my Christian name, always called me Shea, dropping the O from my surname. I hadn't seen Ronan Kiely for probably ten years. I had heard from some of the guys in the Golf Club that he was back in town and, apparently not up to much good. But I had always believed in giving everyone a fair chance, so wasn't overly concerned what others thought.

We exchanged small-talk for a short while and I introduced Ruth and Lisa but Ronan wasn't giving much information away about his life. Then, after a few minutes, his phone rang. Without leaving the table or trying to be discreet he made arrangements to meet someone in Carraig in about half an hour, saying he would grab a taxi or get the bus. As soon as he got off the phone he turned to me saying he had to meet someone to talk about a job, and did I think I might be able to run him over to Carraig?

I took a quick glance at Ruth and in a split second her expression told me in no uncertain terms what my answer should be. Her teeth were tightly clinched and she was imploring me to say *no, to tell him you have an appointment, with a doctor, a dentist, a priest, a pagan, anything. Just say no!* But to my shame, I answered Ruth's unspoken imploring instead of Ronan's brazen question.

'You have to go to the supermarket, don't you dear? I could drop you there and run out to Carraig with Ronan.'

I could tell Ruth was ready to lose it but within five minutes we were on the road. We dropped her off at the supermarket and drove on towards Carraig.

Lisa was happily munching the remains of her muffin, and charming Ronan with her endearing chatter and irresistible smile.

Then he turned to me and said: 'I have to meet this fella in Brook Lawn. If you can wait for me I'll only be a minute and I'll come back to town with you.' Ronan wasn't afraid to ask for favours. What could I say?

He got out of the car and went into no. 8 Brook Lawn Drive. I drove to the end of the road to turn the car while I was waiting for him, and was surprised to see him come running out the gate as arrived back outside the house.

Ronan was shouting as he jumped in. 'Get the fuck out of here, these guys ain't too happy!'

Then I could see a guy running towards us with a baseball bat in his hand. As I pulled away at high speed the bat struck the back of the car and I could see this guy was still running coming. As we came to the junction of Brook Lawn Drive and the Carraig Road our pursuer was only a few meters behind us, still ready to lash out. I was terrified for Lisa's safety in the back.

'All clear this side.' Said Ronan, assuring me there was no traffic coming from my left. Checking only to my right I accelerated across the junction. Instantly we were smashed by a car coming from the left. Everything was in slow motion, like a road safety ad, except it was nightmarishly real. In horror I looked back, and instantly knew my life was changed forever. Lisa had taken the full impact.

The car stopped spinning and I leapt from my seat and went back to her, lifted her out of the car and performed CPR, artificial respiration and screamed at almighty God to bring her back. But she was gone, and with her all our dreams, and hope for a future, and everything we held sacred was gone too.

Five weeks later Ruth had left and returned to her parents in Scotland. She could never forgive me. She couldn't even look at me. I could never forgive myself.

It's now four years since she left I have not seen or spoken to her. I guessed she visited Lisa's grave regularly, because there were often presents left there, especially at Christmas or on other special occasions.

Today would have been Lisa's birthday and, as always, I wondered about what might have been. My thoughts, my torment, my guilt were as vivid today as they had been every day since the accident. Though I visited her grave every day, I could find no comfort. I was no closer to finding peace of mind. No more likely to accept that I could not change the past, and move on with my life. Now standing in silence at her grave, my thoughts were brought back the present, by the sound of gravel crunching under foot as somebody approached on the path behind me. Suddenly, a soft warm hand slipped into my mine, and a soft familiar voice said the words I thought I would never hear.

'Johnny, I want to forgive you'

My heart summersaulted in my chest. We stood and held each other tightly for a long time and cried. Only after did I see the child who was standing beside her, arms wrapped around her mother's leg. Ruth could sense my shock.

'This is your daughter, Shauna. I found out I was pregnant after Lisa died but was too bitter to tell you. I wanted you to suffer. Can you please forgive me for keeping her from you?'

Stepping up

By

John McLoughlin

It had been almost four years since his father left. Life for Paul and his family at number 11 Beechfield Gardens had become more stable, happier. Loving even. Paul was a well-adjusted fifteen year old, taking his studies for his Junior Cert seriously. All round a good kid. Some might say a serious boy. He was good at sport, and was looking forward to an important schools hurling final in the coming week.

Beechfield was a quiet estate, lots of young families, seldom if ever any trouble. Number 11 was a well maintained semi-d, with a nice garden, which was carefully tended by Paul's mum Anna. A new family, the Kelly's, had moved into the adjoining house in the spring. They seemed nice, especially Ruth, and her three young children. But Tom was a bit unfriendly and seemed to be away working a lot. Paul had heard raised voices coming from next door a few times, but never anything more than a few words (one of the disadvantages of living in a semi-d).

Anna and Paul's younger sister, Katie, had left a few hours earlier to take his gran to Sunday night bingo. They would always stay with her for a while after bingo, drink tea, maybe do some jobs around her house. Paul knew they wouldn't be home until late, so after watching some sport on TV he decided to head to bed.

He wasn't long lying down when he heard some noise from next door. It seemed more intense than before. Pulling his pillow tightly around his ears he tried to pretend that nothing unusual was happening. Try as he did to ignore them, the sounds kept coming. Sounds which had been all too familiar in his younger years. Sounds which caused his stomach to cramp with fear. Sounds he hoped he would never hear again. Sounds he had vowed he would never tolerate again.

He heard the sound of furniture scraping on a hard floor, the sound of delph or glass breaking. And he was sitting up in bed when he heard the dull but unmistakable sound of a closed fist striking soft flesh. The cry of pain, the sharp retaliatory smack of open hand on bare flesh, pleading cries of: STOP!

Paul could take no more. Then he heard the children's screams. That was it. He leapt out of his bed, threw on his tracksuit and runners and grabbed his hurl as he raced out of the room.

He went out the back door of his house, scaled the dividing wall and went straight for the back door of number 10. The unlocked door swung open and there in front of him, cowering in a corner on the floor was Ruth with her oldest child in her arms. Tom standing over them, fists clinched, soaked in perspiration. She shouted at Paul to run, but as she did Tom turned, and like a raging bull made a drive towards Paul. As Tom advanced, Paul instinctively brought up the hurl, and with one swift stroke, it was game over, lights out, game set and match. Curtains. Tom's knees buckled and he collapsed unconscious on the floor.

Ruth got to her feet, and in spite of a swollen and bloodstained face she got up and hugged and thanked Paul.

Half an hour later, Anna and Katie arrived home just in time to see Tom being driven away in an ambulance.

Paul was shaking like a leaf when they came into the kitchen. 'I had to stop him, mam, I couldn't let him do what dad did to us'

Winter

A blanket of snow
Like tinsel glistening white, Blue skies and sunshine.

Winter wonderland. How amazing to observe A little red robin chirps.

Frosty the snowman
Black hat, gloves and long blue scarf Buttons in his coat.

Enjoy the bright scene,
Slip, slide, sleigh ride up and down, Don't run, wait your turn.

Peggy Garvey.

Moving House

by

Peggy Garvey

Paudie Byrne and his wife Síle had been in love since their late teens. They got married in 1966 in the church in Ballinrobe, Co. Mayo, on a glorious day. The ceremony was very moving with music that was uplifting - especially the hymn *There is Love*. After their honeymoon in Kerry they settled in their terraced house on the side of the street in Cornmarket, Ballinrobe. They were thrilled they could afford their abode and that emigration was not their lot. They painted the kitchen primrose and their bedroom cobalt blue, a restful colour. The atmosphere in the house was always jolly as they welcomed each of their four children over the next eight years, three girls and a boy, their son being their second child. They were wise and caring parents who knew how to discipline and love their children.

The years passed quickly and when Angela, their first, reached twelve they decided the family needed more space for their individual growing needs. But how could they leave their house filled with such precious, nostalgic memories? It would grieve them all, but practicality had to take precedence over sentimentality. Síle suggested they should write about their happy childhood memories and draw pictures of their life there. This would make a cherished family journal. She did a beautiful spread for Sunday dinner. Angela, who loved cooking, helped. Jim Cusack, their neighbour took family photos of this special occasion and a copy was made for close relatives and neighbours. He even offered to take one of the house, front and back.

Paudie contacted the local auctioneer and started the ball rolling. Liam McGovern knew the tricks of the trade like the back of his hand and people trusted him. He put up a FOR SALE sign and placed a photograph in his office window - indicating the value of the house.

'Where do you intend going?' He asked the couple.

'We hope to buy a house outside the town, a bigger one to accommodate our growing family,' answered Síle.

Angela had gone with her mother to Knock to pray specially for guidance regarding this significant event in their lives, which was not to be taken lightly. The auctioneer queried how soon they wanted to move.

'With any luck we would hope to go in a few months,' responded Paudie. 'The bank manager has a good relationship with us. We have paid our mortgage for fourteen years and have only six years left to go.'

McGovern was an astute operator and declared he might have something suitable on his books. His experience was invaluable. He showed them a photograph of the house and they declared it looked attractive.

'It is on the Lough Mask Road. Has four bedrooms and a well-kept garden plus an outside garage.' He continued. 'And it is considerably larger than yours.'

'We will view it,' Paudie enthused.

These developments were encouraging. The whole family would go the following Saturday on this exciting adventure - for that was how the children experienced it.

A warm welcome awaited them: tea and cakes on the six place kitchen table with Maeve's beautiful china plates, cups and saucers. This surprised the children so they were on their best behaviour as these people seemed posh! The atmosphere was calm and peaceful. The rooms tidy and attractive and the bathroom had delightful pink towels which matched the pale pink tiles on the walls. Everywhere was spotless and the rooms were a suitable size. Plenty of light to disperse gloom was important to them and this house looked cheerful and bright. The children were thrilled to run around the back garden chasing each other.

Could they afford this suitable house? They told the children they would talk to the bank manager to see could he help. 'I can give you money from my piggybank?' Volunteered four year old Siobhán generously! They all laughed but thanked her and gave her a hug for such thoughtfulness. Her savings amounted to ten pence and she often counted it with Máire who loved teaching her.

The bank manager, Mr Casey, sat the couple down in his tidy office containing Irish oak furniture overlooking Cornmarket. Everyone respected this tactful man who treated everyone with good grace. He willingly granted them an extension to their mortgage so that they would continue with the same repayments every month. As they came in the front door the children observed their facial expressions and guessed there was good news. They were all ears.

'We will be moving,' declared their dad with a broad smile.

'How soon?' Asked Peadar.

'Within a month when you get your summer holidays.' Síle answered.

'Hurrah!' They shouted in unison. Now they would be sad to be farther away from their town friends but mam said they could cycle or walk in and out for football and basketball and to spend time with their friends. She pointed out that there was space for games in the new residence and this was a welcome change from the confined space they had in town.

The next day dad said preparations for the great move would begin. They could start by sorting their clothes in separate bundles. Mam said she would place a huge box at the top of the stairs on the landing and they would fold them neatly and tightly for maximum space.

'Discard what you don't want.' She advised. Siobhán was particular about hand-me-downs from her sisters, saying they were shabby, as she was sophisticated, but agreed she would keep a few for gardening. Peadar was quick at making decisions about what he had outgrown and ran out to play as soon as his part was done. Angela was thrilled to make a bundle for Máire who thanked her sincerely. Her older sister was growing fast into a beautiful young lady and enjoyed shopping with her mother. They loved fashion! New clothes would be required by both to celebrate their move to their new abode, in due course. Sile held dresses and blouses up to her in front of the mirror to see what she would place in the Vincent de Paul box. She remembered weddings she had attended and the outfits worn. She smiled to think how fashions change and she thanked the discarded suits for the pleasure they had brought. Inanimate items can bring joy to the heart, she reflected, as she kissed them goodbye.

The following week the phone rang and a voice asked could she speak to Paudie.

'This is Maeve from Lough Mask Road.' She announced.

My God, he thought, what if we are disappointed?

'You might remember us and the house we have for sale….we were looking through the auctioneer's books. We need to downsize as our family have all fled the nest. We also wish to be near everything in Ballinrobe. Would it be possible to view yours?'

Paudie thought this might be a joke, so he replied: 'Are you pulling my leg?'

She reassured him that she was serious.

'Give us a week to make it presentable if you don't mind.' He said.

She understood, especially as there were children involved.

Síle was almost incredulous. What hope was in their hearts now! Could this unprecedented event work out? The children agreed they would work hard to have order and beauty in their home.

They ran to their rooms to do their libraries. Máire and Siobhán working together. They enjoyed exploring books. The baby books would go to their little cousins. Máire always read to her younger sister who could by now make up stories which Siobhán would write for her. The little girl knew the sounds of all the alphabet but could not write words yet. She would be so proud of her story though it was very short. The family would praise her and tell new stories. Paudie's grandfather was a seanchaí from Kerry who could hold people spellbound with his gift of storytelling. This love of stories must continue! Angela's favourite book was "Black Beauty" by Anna Sewell. Peadar always looked at National Geographic with his dad and was very keen on general knowledge. By now the parents were delighted to fill the bin with old newspapers such as "The Western People" and "The Mayo News."

After dinner Sile came to see how they were all doing. She was very pleased and encouraged them enthusiastically. They knew a treat would come later for that was her style. Tea and scones would be served at 3.30p.m, followed by ice cream. Meanwhile Paudie cut the grass and had the flowers and shrubs in exquisite condition. He cleaned the path and shone the knocker on the front door. There was beauty and order emerging.

'We do not need to move at all!' said Máire, joking.

'*You* can stay!' Teased Peadar.

Now they gathered the sentimental stuff and placed the items on the shelves in the sitting room, having gathered them from throughout the house.

'When we tidy up first, it makes us think; when we clean everywhere later, it empties the mind.' She declared. They discarded what was not useful or attractive and all agreed they would not assent to the thought that it might come in handy. More was gathered for the Vincent de Paul and each item, now deemed useless, was thanked. Gratitude and not grief ensued.

During afternoon tea they chatted about their favourite things. Siobhan declared that she liked her doll's house best where she had parties. '

'Kicking football with Dad in the garden is my nicest memory.' Said Peadar.

Angela added: 'I always enjoyed being in goal but tried harder to save for Paudie than for you Dad!' She said with a glint in her eye.

Máire loved her bedroom library where she interacted with the characters in the books who were her friends. Síle and Angela stated that their memories of activities in the kitchen were the most precious, where they cooked, baked, tidied and interacted so much.

Maeve and her husband arrived on Sunday to view their home. The rooms seemed bigger as they had discarded so much including two old chairs from the sitting room. The place was sparkling, all carpets had been hoovered. First of all the viewers were delighted with the appearance of the kitchen, next the attractive sitting room, followed by four nice bedrooms. The bathroom was sparkling white, enhanced by red and white towels and scented soap.

'We are thrilled to find this house and it is not a massive distance from where we live.' Declared Maeve. 'We can meet the auctioneer to see can he oblige both parties.'

Business was done and everything was in order by the following Wednesday.

The holidays arrived and the day for the removal vans was the second of July. The Byrnes agreed to place their furniture in Maeve's garage while the furniture from her house was carried into her new abode.

There was goodwill and cooperation with all hands on deck. The sun shone brilliantly and there was a blue, cloudless sky. Síle and the children placed all the kitchen cutlery in a box in their car. Angela gathered all the towels and sheets in the house and packed them into the big family case for transportation in the car boot. Black bags were used for miscellaneous goods and memorabilia and everything was labelled. Mother drove to their new house on the Lough Mask Road and made a celebratory meal and lit a candle:

Bless this house, O Lord we pray,

Keep it safe by night and day

She sang sweetly.

Beds were placed carefully in the new rooms. They had purchased new sheets and blankets to increase the enjoyment and feeling of freshness. The family was grateful. The whole operation had run smoothly, thanks to meticulous planning and the goodwill of all. They were never so exhausted and no alarm clock was set for the morning as they retired to have the sleep of a lifetime!

A Form of Justice

By

Joe Dowling

Sean Scanlon recalled the conversation with Superintendent John Courtney of the National Drug Task Force. Courtney told him that they had caught the driver of the truck and that had smashed into his wife and daughter. He was tentatively linked to the Hammer McDonough, Mr Big in the Midland Drug World. He remained untouchable and the man ultimately responsible for the deaths of many including his wife and daughter but legally above reproach. The investigation was ongoing he was told.

I should have not reported the movement of drugs from the sea plane that landed on Ballykeeran inner lough that day. I should not have called the guards. I should have told a lie at the trial. I would not be here now in this position if I had, he ruefully thought, and my family would not have been killed.

Months later, silently and bitterly he screwed the silencer onto the muzzle of his rifle. He gently cleaned the lenses of the telescopic sight adjusting the magnification to the maximum. He placed the 4.5mm hollow point round into the breech. From his camouflaged prone position he adjusted the bi-pod legs and sighted the gun and waited, and waited.

Eventually The Hammer McDonough emerged from his house carrying a tray of raw steaks. His face filled the sight picture. Scanlon gave a last look around to ensure that he was alone and he sighted the crosshairs just above the left eye of McDonough's face, 150 metres distant.

McDonough was blissfully tending a barbecue and slugged greedily on a bottle of beer, joking and laughing with his guests. The music and laughter was loud and carried over the fields to where Scanlon lay hidden.

He gently squeezed the trigger and there was a deadened crack as the 4.5mm bullet left the gun at 2,550 feet per second on its deadly journey.

A fraction of a second later McDonough's head disintegrated as portions of scattered grey matter sizzled on the bar-b-q and covered the immediate area in blood and gore. He fell lifelessly backward to the ground. The assembled guests, shocked and stunned, were blanketed in scarlet.

Scanlon didn't wait around. He gathered his equipment and silently exited the hide. He trudged silently across the fields, invisible in his dark clothing and eventually reached Portlick Bay where he secured his rifle to the underside of his boat and disappeared into the night.

Yes, he thought, revenge is a dish that should be always served cold but it still won't bring them back.

April

by

Joe Dowling

Every time I meet her, I look in wonderment and awe at my first little grandchild, April. She came into the world a year ago today, hairless, toothless and bereft of clothing. A heart melting tiny bundle of developing energy, curiosity, smiles and sometimes tears. She grows daily and sometimes, because of the intervals between when I see her, I think her growth and development is more sensational than if I were to see her every day. She is now crawling and is more akin to a puppy than a child as she chases the helpless and bewildered cat endlessly around the sitting room floor, emitting the odd shriek of delight as she closes on her prey. Fortunately, the cat has always eluded her clutches to date but the misses are getting nearer all the time. Always exploring and curious beyond her age, she is currently mesmerised by the television and kneels in front of it trying to understand why she can't stick her head into where the colours and shapes emanate. She peers behind the screen to see who is there talking or where the music is coming from, constantly puzzled. A sponge soaking up information, processing it and retaining what is useful in her memory. Still bereft of hair save a few comical short ginger tufts here and there. With her two new bottom teeth, of which she is immensely proud, she loves to bite upon my finger. The pools of blue that are her eyes and in which I would happily flounder and her smile, how it illuminates my world. Her laughter is music to my ears.

I wonder about what kind of a world she will inherit. How tall she will be, how intelligent and well-adjusted she will become. What will be the lifetime challenges that will confront her? What will be her destiny? I sometimes wish that I could see into her future and protect her from the inevitable trials and tribulations it is the human condition to experience. But then I realise that it is not my place to do such things. It is my duty to support her development in order that she may successfully confront whatever challenges life throws at her and to provide her with the support and the tools necessary to overcome them and to keep them in perspective. No one else can assume that responsibility. She must do it herself and hopefully be a better person because of it.

Having a grandchild is also the first time that I have become conscious of the circle of life, of my own mortality. I realise that I have served my purpose the same way that my parents served theirs. I have witnessed the continuation of the genetic line and like the drone in the beehive, I will be able to pass, happy in the knowledge that my primary purpose has been achieved and I am almost redundant.

The Ballykeeran Oak

By

Joe Dowling

Dropped by a careless squirrel as he scuttled across the land,

I germinated in the spring and thus here I came to stand.

Through the years, I have watched the human form as they travelled along the road,

The rich, the poor and the ignorant, as they laboured with their load,

Oblivious to my form and to the shelter that I laid,

To the furtive fumbling's of the young

As they leaned against my shade.

So now they cut me down

Because I was in the way,

An obstacle, a nuisance, even though I once held sway.

For I was once the Ballykeeran Oak

That stood the test of time,

And now I lie upon the ground felled by the chainsaw's whine.

And though broken and forgotten, I bear them no ill will, no ire,

I will still release the warmth of summer days in the hearth, and in the fire.

Her Birthday

by

Janice Dobbie

Tessa was excited. Tonight was the night. She was going to the Young Farmers club dance at the village hall. Never before had she been allowed to go. Her two older sisters had been on many occasions and come home with great tales of what went on (not that she believed half of what she heard). But this time she was going too. She was now eighteen and nobody was going to stop her. She had planned for weeks. Mother had altered her dress and it was more up to date, it was carefully ironed and now hung on the front of the wardrobe ready for her to slip on this evening. Her shoes were polished until they were gleaming. Father could huff and puff as much as he liked but nothing would stop her. Yes. This would be the night of her life.

At 7.30pm, with dire warnings ringing in her ears, Tessa and her two sisters set off to walk the short distance to the village hall. It was lit up like a merry go round. A few of her friends were already there. She headed for them. Her sisters went in other directions. Suddenly she felt so unsure of herself. Not the excited eighteen year old she had been this morning. Now she was actually here: what was she going to do? The girls decided to get a lemonade and sit together. After quite a while, a voice beside Tessa asked: 'Wanna dance?'

She looked up. A strange face, with a shock of thick brown hair was staring down at her He shifted from one foot to the other, waiting for an answer.

'OK.' She said as she had no other offer.

They took to the floor and for the next few minutes felt excruciating pain as he trod all over her tiny size four feet. All she managed to learn was that he lived in the next village and was an apprentice car mechanic.

As she sat down, she could feel rather than see her sisters swooping down upon her full of questions.

'Who is he?'

'Where is he from?'

'Who are his family?'

'What does he do?'

'I've only just met him, and I'm hardly likely to find out anything if you two keep coming in like a rugby scrum at the end of each dance. Now leave me alone. I came here to enjoy myself.'

Miraculously Danny returned to apologise for hurting her feet and sat beside her for some time.

Now, fifty years on, and looking at the small group around her for her birthday, Tessa smiled contentedly. The family had never thought Danny was good enough for her but together they had fought and won. He still could not dance. Life had had its ups and down but basically it had been good and with three children and six lovely grandchildren, Tessa thought: 'We have a lot to be thankful for, when we have each other.'

Big Brother

By

Janice Dobbie

I catapulted into his well organized world when he was all of eight years old. I am not quite sure just what impact I made on him at the time. This information did not come to me until many years later. As a baby I was quite oblivious to the fact of how I had just turned his world upside down!

Being the first child, and indeed a son, he was the most loved and cared for. And after my mother suffered a miscarriage and was told she could have no more children, it seemed that he would be an only child and was indeed more precious than ever.

He enjoyed this wonderful existence, where he had first call on the attention of both parents, doted on by grandparents, and having no competition for anything for some time. However this immediately changed, eight years later, when I noisily entered his world and, small though I was, changed everything, knocking him for six!

I was a baby. I was a girl. I couldn't go fishing with him. I couldn't play with his Mecanno. I couldn't play with his Airfix set. As far as he was concerned I was absolutely useless. When he came home it was either to hear *"Ssh, the baby's sleeping…"* Or *"…Not now, I'm feeding the baby.…"* Or perhaps *"…the baby needs changing."*

The baby always needed something. He no longer had first call on parent's time, especially Mother. So he decided I had to be useful for something but he just had to figure out what.

And that is exactly what he did.

When I had grown up a little, he asked me to help him in various things. One day he asked me to go to the corner shop for him. He was now a teenager. I went in and asked for a packet of Stella salt.

The grocer looked at me strangely and then kindly asked: 'Who sent you for that?'

'My big brother.'

'I think you'd better tell him to come and get it himself.' He said smiling.

'I can't do that. He told me not to come back without it.'

'You just tell him it's too heavy for you.'

I sighed, not understanding at all. Then he said: 'Stella salt comes from the local salt mines but they have been closed for years. Jim is having you on.'

I was furious and marched straight back home to tell him so. When I did he laughed at me and the more he laughed the more angry I became. A red faced seven year old child, with blonde curls bobbing in anger must have been a real sight for his sore eyes. I just couldn't win. And this was only one of his many pranks and of course I fell for them each and every time.

On the whole we got on not too badly although we did have some fierce arguments. However they always cleared the air about various matters.

The other occasion which springs to mind is that of his wedding. As this was to be my one and only likely time to be a bridesmaid I was most excited. However as plans were revealed my excitement gradually waned. My thoughts had been of me in a beautiful dress walking down the aisle behind the bride, smiling serenely in a crowded church. Reality proved to be very different. Bride and groom were a rather private pair and did not want a lot of fuss. They planned to marry in the home of a friend so obtained a special licence for a Friday evening. I was to come straight home from college, change, and make my way to the venue with my parents. The only guests were the friends in whose home the ceremony was held, a niece of the bride, bride's mother, my parents and myself plus the minister who would conduct the wedding. Not at all what I had expected. To top it all Mother made the bride's and bridesmaid's dresses not out of beautiful shiny fabric but they were hostess gowns, as was the style of the day, made out of polyester fabric. I was most disappointed.

Afterwards, we made our way to a local hotel for a quiet meal. When I spoke to my brother many years later, his reply was: 'It was my wedding, not yours, so I could do as I wished.'

When I was about fourteen he almost broke my heart. I was a great showband fan and he, being older, would go with his girlfriend to various dance halls to hear the different bands. At this particular time my favourite, *The Royal* with Brendan Bowyer, were coming to the Flamingo Ballroom in Ballymena and Jim and his girlfriend were going. I was thrilled to bits because he had promised to take me with them. I didn't see any problem, for the Flamingo was one of the most respectable ballrooms in the country. The lads even had to wear a tie to get in! (Mind you, I have since heard many stories of how one tie could be used for over twenty lads!)

As the night drew near I couldn't sleep for thinking about it. I had all the singles. I could do the *Hucklebuck* perfectly. My father said if I didn't stop playing it he would go out and find Brendan Bowyer and personally strangle him to stop him singing. I did everything with extra vigilance, all homework was perfect. I went to bed early to have more time to dream about the evening. I wanted nothing to stand in the way of my big night.

On the evening, I had just had dinner, went to my room, washed and changed and was coming downstairs to be ready in good time. I collided with my mother as she brought some towels upstairs. She took one look at me, eyeing me up and down from head to toe, and immediately said: 'What are you all dressed up for?'

'I'm going out.'

'Where?'

'To see *The Royal* with Jim.'

'Oh no you are not.'

'But he said he would take me with him!'

'Where is he now?'

'I don't know.'

'Well you can be sure of this. No daughter of mine is going to see a showband at fourteen years of age. You can go and take that get up off right now.'

'But he promised . . . '

'It doesn't matter what he promised. I'm promising you now: You are not going.'

She pushed by me on the stairs and I sat right there where I was and sobbed. I sobbed and sobbed until the physical pain was so bad I thought my heart would literally break in two. That was my first experience of heartbreak and nothing had prepared me for it.

I sat out on those stairs until well after 10p.m. Weeping, hiccupping, alternating between bouts of disappointment, heartbreak and anger. Sometimes directed at my mother, sometimes at my brother, but all I knew for sure was I could not see Brendan Bowyer. My father came out and suggested I listen to some of my records, but I was beyond that. I said: 'But Dad, I just want to be there to SEE him. His eyes are SO beautiful.'

He left me at that, and I vaguely remember sometime later, someone carrying me upstairs and laying me on my bed for the night.

When I next saw my brother, I was not angry, nor furious, but heartbroken. He had brought me a new record personally signed: *To Janice, from Brendan B…* but even so, I did not speak to him for a long time. It hurt. What he had done to me hurt a lot. It was a joke to him but he had hurt his little sister a great deal, possibly more than he could ever have imagined. We eventually made up and when we spoke of it (about 40 years later) he said: 'Sure, I only said I'd take you because I knew you'd never be allowed to go.'

Many years have passed since those days. We have both changed but in some ways we are both the same. I am and always will be his little sister. He rings me often and sometimes in the middle of a call will say: 'How does a wee girl like you know a big word like that?'

On the other hand when I have big decisions to make, it is to him that I turn, to talk things through. I now see in him things which I see in myself and for that reason we are closer now than ever. Both of us are in the autumn years of life now and realize we have fewer years ahead than have gone before. We make the most of the time left to us. He is my very own big brother and I wouldn't change him for the world.

Death of a Future

By

Raphael O'Brien

I sat at the side of the hospital bed holding my wife's hand. I was in a daze as our beautiful bundle of joy, Baby Nadine was passed from nurse to doctor in a flash. The air of tension that abounds alerts us to the fact that all is not as it should be.

Why are we not being told anything? Something is wrong. Christ not our baby!

'Page the consultant paediatrician on call!' Shouted the head nurse overseeing our birth. The junior doctor at the end of the bed is panic stricken; clearly out of his depth. He hastily confers with the midwife who summoned him just minutes earlier.

My wife Mary is ashen faced now not knowing where to look. I try hastily in vain, to engage her in conversation, or even make eye contact. Anything to ease her mind.

But I myself am lost for words.

The gravity of the situation overcomes my wife.

'Ah fuck it's all too much Tom I can't.' She said, breaking down as she sobs loudly on my shoulder.

Female intuition seemed to tell my wife more than words or doctors could express. 'I just get a sense that they're not telling us the full story.'

'Ah now, Mary. Don't be fretting love, it may not be that serious. The nurse would have said if there was anything major. It's only precautions.'

It's amazing how optimistic and resourceful a first time father can be in a situation like this. Holding my wife's wedding ring with my fingers, her head on my shoulder; I tried to come up with ever more novel ways to defuse the tension in the room and ease the stress which my wife must be feeling.

Soon, I am at sixes and sevens. Really out of my depth as I try to grapple with the possible severity of what this could mean for our baby Nadine. The nurse has left the room, leaving her colleague holding the post.

I look at my watch frantically. 7.45pm. Nadine was born nearly half an hour ago and we still had no answers. Every parents worst nightmare.

The young student doctor checking our little girl's vital signs silently without a word only adds to the tension. *Where is the real doctor! Not Some School Girl! Why aren't we being told anything?*

The ward door opens hastily. The midwife has arrived back with help. A senior doctor who appears to be about mid forties.

Immediately assuming the level of command warranted of his pay grade. He looked at Nadine. Read her chart. Seemed to come to a conclusion and turned to us coldly and said the one phrase everybody in our situation dreads:

'Mrs. Murphy, I'm sorry but...'

The rest of the conversation floored us. We were expecting some problems, but this was more severe than Mary or I had ever thought possible.

The doctor called it: Congenital Rubella Syndrome.

Mary had contracted Rubella before her pregnancy and we were told that there was an 85% chance the infant would go on to develop the disease. With that news, our little bundle of joy's entire future seemed left to chance like a sick lottery.

The doctor now started barking orders at the staff in a frantic manner; clearly distressing Mary.

'What's wrong love? Why aren't we being told anything else? What's going on?'

'It's just precautions. The doctors have it under control. Just relax.'

I was trying to appear calm in a desperate attempt to placate Mary. Inwardly though I was frantic. Screaming silently.

This cannot be happening again! An Ectopic pregnancy. Three miscarriages. Now this Fuckin Shite! It's a bleedin' Nightmare. God knows best my eye!

The doctor now conferred with his maternity team for what seemed like an eternity.

This fuckin can't be good.

Suddenly, I felt Mary nudge my arm. 'Why, aren't we being told anything? This is a nightmare!'

'I know, love,' I said, gently wiping her fevered brow with a damp towel. 'But they really are doing their best'

Our precious little Nadine is now attached to a multitude of tubes, and strange machines before being whisked out the door. Moments later the consultant returns alone.

'Mrs. Murphy, Your little girl is stable now. However, she is very fragile, and we are doing everything in our power. We still need to confirm if it's Congenital Rubella Syndrome.

'Is this like the MMR, Doctor?' Mary asks. And then: 'It's my fault; isn't it?

"Try to relax, Mrs. Murphy. We will know more after further tests. Please be patient We are doing all we can.'

Mary exploded after the consultant left.

'It's all shit, Tom. How could Mum be so set in her ways? If she had just got me the fuckin injection this wouldn't be happening. Now our little angel is…' Unable to finish, she sobbed quietly.

'Don't be jumping to the worse outcome, please Mary.'

'She's three pounds nothing, Tom! With the possibility of poor hearing, not to mention learning problems. Feels like a death to me. Where is our ray of light or hope? Poor Little Nadine.'

Nadine's bloods were sent to lab for further testing. Forty eight hours they said. So short and yet a lifetime. Little Nadine's future was in God's hands now. All we could do was Wait, hope and pray.

Married just three years, Mary and I live with her parents in the village of Tyrellspass. An hour commute from work in Dublin and Ballinasloe respectfully. We are saving for a deposit. Mary is a lab technician. I work in a digital marketing firm.

Our own home. It was like a dream. A place with a garden where our children could have room to play. Somewhere to raise a family in peace and serenity. Right now though, none of this mattered. A house and garden seemed like a fairytale. A fantasy away from our present nightmare. But at least being able to visualise this picture provided some sort of freedom from our new reality.

It was now time for Nadine's Six Week Checkup. A parent's worst nightmare could not begin to describe how we felt. Words fail to describe emotions in a situation like this. It is all too overwhelming. It felt like a death of a close relative. Though NOT the Death of Nadine; we still grieved nonetheless. It was the death of her future! The death of her precious healthy childhood. And we pined in silence.

Mary initially chose the name Nadine before birth. But we were both in unison that the name was immensely significant now as it meant *hope* and *love*. Two things that were vital in our lives just then.

The young doctor pulled no punches today.

'There is no easy way to say this but your baby's pupils are not reacting. It may signify blindness. More tests are needed. We will know more soon.'

Next the doctor checked her hearing. We had noted that our baby didn't seem bothered by noise. We hoped we were wrong but the diagnosis was stark.

'Mr. Murphy. Your daughter is deaf and dumb. There is also the inevitable issue of learning difficulties. The diagnosis has been confirmed as Congenital Rubella Syndrome.'

Mary remained mute. Shocked by the reality of the situation. My reaction was Polar Opposite and I fished for further details but it didn't change anything. Soon, the appointment was over.

Eventually the big day came. Our precious little Nadine was given the green light to go home. We were overjoyed. It was a day we thought would never come.

First thing first, we held a celebration for close family and friends but after this; day to day went by slowly. Milestones came and were missed on several occasions. However, gradually with care and patience, the memorable day came when little Nadine uttered her first words that will be forever etched in my mind.

'DADA MILK'!

Mary and I couldn't believe our ears. It was a day we thought would never come! It was a day we thought we would never see. And coming as it did on the day of Nadine's final heart checkup in Crumlin hospital.

As Nadine progressed, Mary and I agonised over her starting school. She favoured *Special Needs* while I held the opposite view. Eventually the assessments were conclusive and I got my wish. Nadine started Junior Infants at our local school in Tyrellspass. She made many friends and, with the exception of some remedial lessons, was treated no different than any other classmate.

Today Mary and I are speechless as we watch our precious angel make her First Communion. A milestone we thought we would never see. Even our daughter's notions of a stretch limo for her special day doesn't seem such a big deal now!

Her mother's reaction says it all: 'Ah God Tom! Get Real. She's eight. She really has you wrapped around her baby finger!'

In Search of a Ghost

by

Oliver J Higgins

At the rear of our homestead there was an old empty two storey house which had been lived in by two ladies named Mary and Nanny. I never knew them as they had passed away some years before my birth. It was now owned by a very amicable farmer who lived a few miles away.

For safety reasons he had a sign on the gate that said:

NO TRESPASSING!

Despite the sign, my sisters and I used to go out there to play.

We climbed in through one of the windows on the ground floor. We sometimes heard the sound of the owner's car coming and this made us flee quickly before getting caught. Our mother always knew where to find us when we were missing. She always warned us not to go out there anymore and gave us a bit of a telling off. She promised not to tell our father if we agreed not to go there again. This went well for a while but temptation summoned us and off we headed to make another visit. Lo and behold, her patience grew thin, she made good on her threat and told our father. He gave us a right telling off. We were under strict instructions not to go there anymore. He said that there were ghosts out there and he seen long white-haired Nanny looking out the parlour window and Mary was peering from the bedroom window upstairs as recently as the previous night. That gave us something to think about for a while.

However, one windy day, curiosity overcame me. I was feeling brave and adventurous and went in search of a ghost. I decided to go on the voyage alone. A little bit of fear was grappling me but I continued on my journey. I gently climbed through the window and carefully looked around. There were noises and whistling coming from the wind which I did not pay any heed to. I entered the parlour and looked into a press. There was nothing of interest there except a few old empty bottles. Then I proceeded to explore the kitchen and the dairy. There was an old open fireplace in the kitchen with a massive wide chimney where I could see the sky when I looked up. The dairy was a little room off the kitchen but there was no sign of anyone or anything. Becoming a bit braver I now proceeded upstairs to pursue my investigations.

There were two rooms which were small and pokey. The ceilings had partly the same slope as the roof. Each room had a wallpress, a bed and a dressing table. I searched the one at the top of the stairs first - in the press and under the bed but there was no sign of anyone or anything. I then cautiously entered the last room and peered into the press and found it empty. I was about to inspect under the bed when I heard a loud noise. It was like a bang accompanied by a screeching, crying noise. That's when I got the fright of my life!

I fell into the empty bed with the shock, not knowing what to do. There was a damp old smell in the room and the bed felt really musty. I heard the noise again; fear really had me in its grips as I lay there helpless not knowing what was going to happen. I could neither laugh nor cry. My heart was in my mouth, thumping at an awful rate as I lay there flummoxed. My energy was beginning to sap. I heard the noise once more which, by now, was getting louder and the screeching sharper.

'They are going to get me……and God only knows what they will do to me!'

As I lay there helpless, I began feeling that my life was in danger and I began to regret that I did not follow my parents advice. I then fell into a deep sleep began having frightening nightmares.

Suddenly, I had an urge to go to the toilet and was afraid I was going to wet the bed. Then I heard someone calling out frantically. It sounded like my mother's voice with my sisters who were lamenting my disappearance. "Ollie?! Where are you?! Are you alright?" Then I woke up with a start and came to my senses. I think I answered back: 'I'm Ok!' And then I stood up and shook myself properly awake and looked around. The wind had ceased by now and it was calm.

The banging door had stopped, the cringing hinges had ceased, and there were no funny noises anymore. And no more ghosts.

Never too late to Educate

by

Oliver Higgins

In life you are never too old or too late.

At any stage you can change your ways and a new life you can create.

We all have a choice today.

In our comfort zones we do not have to stay.

Take some action, endure some change.

Our lives and ways of living we can rearrange.

With your mind and brain you can always educate.

By doing so you can excel and graduate.

By applying yourself you will be enduring some assertiveness.

Of many new values you will inherit alertness.

Our past experience is what got us to where we are today.

When you enjoy what you do each day; it is not work it is play.

A personal profile is all about what we do, think, and see.

Really and truly it's about the past and the present about me.

All about morals and values, good and bad.

Likes, dislikes, beliefs, disbeliefs and if we are happy or sad.

It's about how we approach and live each day.

Keeping positivity up front and negativity out of our way.

For a good life and true living now I really yearn.

Always remember during your lifetime you are never too old, or too late to learn.

Harold's Letter

By

Marva Fitzpatrick

Dear Dr. Rice,

Firstly, I must apologise for the kaleidoscope of colours presented in the print on these pages. It seems that I find myself indebted to the kindness of a ten year old boy these days. His name is Omar. And I met him when his renegade football presented me with the opportunity. My voice responded to the unfamiliar sound of him rustling beneath my window, left subtly ajar for the purpose of ventilation. It was a trial at first, to gain trust, but a carefully nurtured series of conversations over a period of three months has resulted in me finding an ally. He tells me he wants to be a surgeon, like his Dad, and it does not take much imagination to foresee this reality in his future. I am drawn to the empathetic intonations of his voice and the surprising attention to my wellbeing. It is how I find myself in possession of a pen that changes colours at a click and a small writing pad which is compatible with a cathartic view of my world.

My room, which was once occupied by my brother, Harold, is sufficient, I suppose. Not too clean but not excessively dirty either. Although, I have always been familiar with the house, this silence has allowed for an acute intimacy with its incessant hubbub. A flustered Annabelle, my daughter, is in the kitchen at present so I know that it is five in the afternoon. The clatter of a saucepan or the chop of an obstinate vegetable usually commences an hour before *his* arrival. My pension finances this fine eating with fresh fillets of sirloin served every Thursday following a trip to the post office.

'Where's my pension?!' I shout through the slight opening in the door.

'Mam…please stop…if he hears you, there will be hell to pay.'

'I haven't seen a penny of it since that fat fucking slob moved in…. what is it?… Over five years ago now if I remember. Have you married him yet?'

'No,' she whispers. 'He is doing an interview next week.'

'A fucking interview…. that fella wouldn't work off a battery.'

'Mam…. please…be careful….Dan will be home soon.'

'Fuck him and fuck you…eating your big steaks while I am left to eat chopped liver or chicken…. or most likely *dog*.'

'It is *not dog*,' she sighs. 'The butcher simply minced your chicken…. on account of your dentures…not fitting. Remember?'

'Liar,' I whisper.

Truth is I don't often engage in these outbursts as it results in an earlier curfew for a locked door. When he does arrive I am concealed like an ugly government secret while he is taken to the living room further down the hall to indulge in a lavish meal. Sometimes they will sojourn upstairs for their barbaric conjugal rights. I not only hear the assortment of groans and snorts but the inherent uncomfortable humiliation of my daughter also. Still it is hard to feel pity for the sycophantic drivelling mess she has become. Just like her uncle, Harold.

I think about Harold when the sizzling steak and fried onions is exciting my taste buds every Thursday. It is the day he visits your office, Doctor, where he vigilantly keeps his weekly four o'clock appointment without fail. I know by now that you have grown fond of him as most of the community have. When I frequented the shops I would often overhear a warm greeting for him. Something like: '*Hey Harold, how are you? You're looking well…. They must be treating you like a king in Mary Mercers?*'

Following a hyena like laugh, Harold would give a little skip of delight. '*They brought me to see Johnny Cash last night….*' He would slur through compressed lips and projectile saliva. His incapacitated hand was always held aimless against his chest, his right foot awkwardly turned in perpetual greeting with his left one.

The conversation about tribute acts would become animated but the underlying sense of protection and kindness that was extended to my brother was apparent. It was always how it had been for Harold. Even before his crumpled body was found at the bottom of the stairs.

Harold always walked up the stairs on the left hand side much like Annabel when she is intrepidly following Dan. In both cases it is a painstaking exercise for different reasons. Harold liked to count the steps. Counting, counting, counting all the way up. Two steps up was good. Three was bad. When my mother cajoled him to use both sides of the banisters his body would freeze as he agitatedly mumbled about 'germs' and 'diseases'. Hands had to be washed. Windows checked. Hands washed. Doors checked. Hands washed. Until the medication disseminated to the correct region of the brain and he would finally succumb to sleep leaving an exhausted, dishevelled mother in his wake. I only remember a brewing resentment for Harold, possibly as a result of his time-consuming behaviours. Indeed, in the period of twenty years of his tenure in this house I do not remember my mother ever asking after my welfare. Her interactions with me were usually demanding for more help or accusatory in nature.

'Harold has another bruise on his arm. Where did he get that?' She asked me again one morning as I hastily scoffed a slice of toast.

'Probably school,' I answered. 'You know there *are places* where Harold is hated!'

I can tell you, Doctor, that I didn't stay too long in her company following the ensuing shriek of disbelief.

My mother is in the room with me most nights now. She was always an oddly discrete woman, so her appearances usually follow my visit to the bucket left inside the door. Annabelle empties it after the piece of lard has left for wherever he goes every day. On Wednesdays , Annabelle might even give me a bed bath but it is not sufficient to deter the grease in my hair or the black grime beneath my fingernails. On one dark and hazardous journey to the fancy lavatory, I hit my shin bone off the edge of the bed. I had to use the duvet to stem the never ending gush of blood that continued through the evening. Perhaps my moans unearthed my mother's restless spirit but as I turned to find my way into the bed, I noticed her standing above me staring at my anguished state with sullen eyes.

'How does it feel to have created a monster?' She asks

'I didn't create a monster,' I say. 'I created fodder for the monster.... *big* difference.'

She is standing at the back wall now, looking bored with my plight.

'Which one did you create, Mother?' I whisper.

'Both!' she shrieks with laughter before dissipating before my eyes.

It has been a week since I injured my leg, Doctor. The area is swollen and red, a light yellow pus has stained my pyjamas. Annabelle is distracted. Dan is drunk almost every evening, his demands insatiable. I cannot bear to hear her whimpering acquiescence to him but it is an integral part of who she is. I have counted eleven apologies in one hour, at least six were uttered to me. Omar has disappeared for a number of days and I fear this letter will lie forgotten. An exhaustion has assailed my body compelling it to copious rest. Lardy Dan is in the kitchen now, I can hear him opening the fridge and slurping the milk directly from the carton.

'How was your day?' Annabelle whines.

'Fine.' He grunts.

'My mother is ill.'

'What's wrong with her?'

'She has a fever…she is not really making any sense.'

'Jaysus…as if she ever did,' he sneers. 'She was always a mad bitch…. you'd be best not to listen to her…these things run in families, you know. You hardly expect me to stay married to a crazy, do you?'

'No. I suppose not.'

For a long time, the only sound in the kitchen was wood against steel, stirring.

I went to see Harold in Mary Mercers once. It was after our mother died. But I am certain that this information has already been reported to you, Doctor. I stood in the reception area for a good twenty minutes before they sent their most officious (and I suspect intimidating) nurse manager to me. You probably know the one I am talking about. She stood solid before me, eyes slanted with a compressed smile dividing her face. Her unruly red hair was barely contained by a black scrunchie which looked like it belonged to a daughter. Her stare remains fixed on mine and I can see the remnants of a sleepless night accentuating sunken hazel eyes.

'What can I do for you?' she clipped.

I extend my hand towards her but she barely touches my fingers.

'I am Mary Sharpman, Harold's sister.' I say.

I know who you are,' she answers looking at me quizzically. 'Harold does not wish to see any visitors today.'

'Oh, okay……I have some of his things from the house.'

I take a snow globe, a lighter and a book from a bag. She looks at the paltry offerings and with a smile I hear her say. 'Thank you. I will make sure he gets them. But I am obliged to tell you that Harold has specifically asked not to see you ever again. I am sure you understand that Harold sustained a significant head injury. It is our duty to make sure that he does not become too agitated.'

'I am sure you cannot stop me from seeing my brother, nurse?'

'Harold has been professionally assessed for capacity, Mrs. Sharpman. And passed with flying colours. This means that he fully understands what is being said to him and what he is saying to others. The injury did leave deficits but his cognition, I can assure you, is intact.'

'Who ordered these tests?'

'Dr Rice.' She answered smugly.

I always found them to be a weak breed. Nurses I mean. Their constant need for validation from the higher echelons of society irked me. She folded her arms now, glancing at a pager secured to a top pocket of her uniform, willing it to beep. When it did, I watched her indulged arse waddle away from me with a determined step. Words of caution to the rest of the staff already forming on her lips. The decision to write this letter formed in my mind from that very moment.

Omar returned yesterday, much to my relief. I am reinvigorated to look for the letter under my pillow, clicking my pen to red ink. Shortly after this discussion at Mary Mercers I disappeared from view, partly owing to the changed circumstances I have explained. I am sure now this is why the intimations I perceived that day may have subsided somewhat. Harold had a memory that was solely stimulated by a meeting with distressful situations or individuals. The memory of me would be stale in busy minds. My fever is unyielding now, the sweat has drenched my bed clothes. My mother stands over me goading me to finish the letter. Annabelle is distraught also but I tire of her unrelenting apologies. I have instructed Omar to return when the smell of steak is rife in the air.

He is to take this letter to you immediately ensuring its arrival at four o'clock on Thursday. You must read it to Harold when he arrives for his appointment. I can see him naively smiling as you read. The involuntary movement of his head deepening with each word until the bobbing motion requires your attention. Harold will finish my sentences as you read, as he has always been prone to. You will instruct your receptionist to make him tea and he will manipulate your afternoon as he is accustomed to. The words will be sharp to the ear and I am certain that within the repertoire of emotions both of you feel; pity for me will not be one.

And here is most likely why: We did move Harold to this downstairs room eventually. My room. It was a larger, brighter, carefully furnished haven in comparison to the upper rooms. My mother seemed convinced that removing the stress of climbing stairs every day would help his condition. It resulted in a temporary reprieve. Instead he fixated each week on a new obsession. The flower pattern on the kitchen tile or the clanking of a saucepan when preparing meals. Each new fetish deepening my mother's unconditional devotion to her son's needs.

'He cannot help it, Mary,' she would say. 'Can you not understand that he is ill?'

The burning resentment within me seemed to fester at this time. So every day when we were alone I would insist that he tackle the stairs again and again. I would scream at him when he counted. I would force his hands to grip the banisters. I would block his access to any sinks. He whimpered and cried, rocking his frame back and forth as if in an imaginary cradle. You say he has capacity, Doctor, but I am sure that the only event Harold will truly remember is my penultimate act of anger and frustration. One day I managed to get him to grip both sides of the banister. I screamed at him to move. He remained frozen, wailing in fear. I became enraged and raised my leg to position my dominant foot between his shoulder blades. All the accusations, the lack of empathy, the lack of attention, the maternal looks of disdain forced the movement of that foot against his back until he landed in that contorted space at the bottom of those stairs.

So now, Doctor, the sepsis in my blood will soon have completed its journey. And if not, perhaps you want me committed to a psychiatric unit? Either way I win. Dying holds no fear for me. Life now is all a prison. A prison here with Annabelle and Dan, or an official prison with a purpose. I'll take three good meals a day from you, no problem. Warm clean bed clothes. My pension delivered to me. All because I kicked Harold down the stairs? Sounds absolutely perfect. So perhaps it may be time to reach for the phone, doctor? As is your duty, and my last chance for a better life.

Alice

By

Chantalle Loughran

All Mary could hear was her heavy breathing under the duvet. Panicked and sweaty, she was terrified her husband Peter would hear her, and know she was awake. He carried out his usual morning routine - making coffee and showering. After what seemed an eternity, she finally heard his footsteps walk towards the front door. But today there was a pause. She shut her eyes and held her breath as she heard him come back upstairs to get his laptop. He stood in the room and examined her, hoping to find her awake. When he was satisfied with his assumption that she might still be asleep, he went back downstairs. As the front door opened, the sweet sound of birds was sharply muted by the banging of the door. She knew he would be annoyed that she wasn't awake to make him breakfast. But she didn't care anymore. She was finally alone, and she was safe. She had a plan, and for now that was some hope.

Needing visual reassurance, she ran to the window and peaked behind the blinds to watch him drive out of the gates. She sighed with relief. She knew she would have sixty minutes before he would call her to check up on her, so she immediately got to work. She went first to the loose floorboard in the spare bedroom and took out her money, fake passport with her new name on it, Alice Ryan, and her brown wig. Then she hastily got dressed in her disguise and hurried downstairs, cleaning up every step of the way so she wouldn't leave a trace of evidence.

She felt confident her plan would work. Her wig and tracksuit completely transformed her usual appearance. He always insisted she wore dresses and high heels. Even at home. It was exhausting, but she was nearly free of him. Her new clothes that she had bought had been hidden in her wardrobe for weeks now, and she lived in fear that he might find them. But he hadn't. She made sure to remove his favourite dress and matching heels from her wardrobe to take them with her, as she was sure he would later notice they were gone. If he was going to report her as a missing person, she wanted the police to look for a blonde wearing a pink dress with nude heels, not a brunette wearing a khaki tracksuit.

When she was ready to leave, she looked at herself in the long mirror in the hallway. She barely recognised her reflection, yet this made her happier than she had been in weeks. She reminded herself that she was leaving Mary behind and taking on her new identity as Alice. Alice was brave and clever, much stronger than Mary. Now that she was Alice, she knew she would be fine. Taking a last look behind her, she headed off towards the train station. It was raining, which was perfect, as she could cover her head with a hood and umbrella. She would be practically invisible in this weather. She set off towards her freedom. She made her way through the busy estate and down the laneway past the church. She knew she had to take the long route in order to avoid any possibility of CCTV. Thank goodness her husband's security cameras were fake or she may never have been able to leave the grounds.

Once she arrived at Athlone station, she reminded herself to be careful as she might bump into her brother-in-law, Simon, on his way to work. She pulled her hood as far forward as she was able, put on a pair of pink sunglasses and walked towards the platform with her head down. Her mouth was dry, and her heart raced as she stood there. Despite the anonymity she had amongst the numerous morning commuters, she knew that this was where it could all go wrong. There were cameras, and Athlone was so small that you were always bound to meet a neighbour or a familiar face. She knew once she stepped on the train that she could find a seat and hide behind a book, but until then she remained on edge.

As she looked up to buy her ticket, she could see Simon in the corner of her eye. And he wasn't alone. Her body froze with fear when it dawned on her that the dark figure beside him seemed familiar. All of a sudden she could smell him. His old spice aftershave made her stomach flip. She looked over and confirmed to herself that it was Peter. But what was he doing at the train station? Why hadn't she seen his car outside? Possibly because she wasn't looking for it. Where had he been for the last hour? At *6.30am?* He normally went to the gym *after* work, and he had showered before he left the house. It didn't make sense. Maybe he was meeting his gym instructor *Gabby* again. They had always had a suspicious relationship at best.

He hadn't spotted her, but she knew it was only a matter of time. And so she did the only thing she could do. She left the station and abandoned her plan. As she walked through the old doors of the station and out into the cold air, tears began to fill her eyes. She was now without hope. She put her hand to her stomach and felt a tremor of guilt, and a feeling of failure. Just as she was about to head home, she looked up and watched a bus driver climb into the Tullamore bus, about to close the doors behind him. Reminding herself that Alice was strong and brave, she too jumped onto the bus. She could find a way to get to Dublin Airport from Tullamore. She had time to spare. She had allowed for any unforeseen delays.

As she sat down the back of the bus, she scanned the car park for Peter's car. It was parked in the far corner. He was still close by. There was still a chance he could leave the station and spot her on the bus. Her sixty minutes were almost up. She only had a few minutes left before he would call her mobile, which was still at the house, to check in on her. And when she didn't answer, she was certain he would leave the station and go straight home.

She didn't dare to move as she waited for the bus to fill up. It was 7:28am. Could he be calling her phone *before* the train arrived? If so, he'd definitely know something was up. She still couldn't hear the sound of the train on the tracks, so she knew he would still be standing on the platform. But for how much longer?

All of a sudden she was distracted when she felt a hand touch her on her shoulder. The panic made her feel ill and faint. She looked up to see a nice older man asking her if he could sit beside her, and she began to calm herself. She shuffled up against the window - praying that she wouldn't be seen. She hadn't been a practicing Catholic since she was a child, but she had already said three prayers in the last week alone. One was that he wouldn't hit her on her face, so that she could easily disguise herself without having any distinguishing marks. The second was that he wouldn't find her disguise, passport, or runaway money. The third was that she would be able to escape before the morning phone call. The next few minutes would test her reformed faith.

She felt a strong metallic taste in her mouth, the all too familiar symptom she had been enduring for the last couple of weeks. As she drank the water she had brought, her stomach began to feel queasy, and she was worried she would vomit all over the older man beside her. *Why was the bus taking so long to leave?*

Then she heard it, the hissing of the doors closing. She could calm herself ever so slightly. She was getting closer to her safety. As the doors closed, and the bus accelerated, she kept her eyes glued to the station doors. Just as the bus drove away, she spotted Peter on his phone. He looked angry, but he couldn't see her. He wouldn't see her. *I might just make it*, she thought.

The Ghostbuster

By

Chantalle Loughran

Matthew looked out his kitchen window at the beautiful sunshine and decided to sit outside in the glorious morning weather to enjoy his coffee. As he was about to take his place on his swing chair, he was distracted by James, the little boy next door. James was sitting on the pavement with his arms folded and his legs crossed. He had clearly been crying and was rubbing his eyes. Matthew, being a caring avuncular type of man, walked over to him to check on him.

'Good morning, James. Are you working on your suntan?' He opened.

'No, I'm not. I'm angry at my mum. She won't believe me about the man.' James replied angrily.

'Some things can be hard to believe James. What exactly did the man do?'

'He's a ghost. And he keeps showing up in my room at night. My mum won't listen.'

'Maybe she's never seen a ghost and doesn't know that they really exist. The only people I know who believe in ghosts, are people like you and I who've seen them. Tell me about this ghost.' He said, as he sat down on the pavement beside him.

'He's got a long scary face, and he appears every night in my room, on the wall.'

'Does he say much? Or is he just visiting?'

'He doesn't say anything, he just stares at me.'

'Hmmm, I wonder is he a friendly ghost?'

'No, he has a cross face.'

'Oh dear, well that doesn't sound nice. Maybe he's just sad because he's a ghost. Some ghosts don't like being ghosts. You should try and chat to him.'

'He's too scary. I don't like him. I just want him to go away!'

'Everyone is scary before you get to know them. You'd be afraid of me if you didn't know me. Maybe, he's even frightened of you. Try and talk to him tonight. You could tell him if he doesn't like your room that he can always leave, like they do in that Ghostbusters movie.'

'Ok. I'll give it a go' James said reluctantly.

Since the weather was so lovely, Matthew had his gardener Fred come over to his house. Fred spent the whole day working in the yard, cutting back all the hedges and some of the taller trees by the side of the house. Matthew had been meaning to get this done for quite some time. He was concerned that the trees would cast a shadow onto his neighbours' house and they would lose the lovely sunshine in their back garden. It was only as he sat in his swing chair that evening, admiring his newly trimmed hedges, that it dawned on him that James' bedroom was on the same side of the house as his many trees. With this thought he immediately let out a loud jubilant laugh. He knew that James would sleep well tonight, as it occurred to him, he had not only created James' ghost, but that he could also officially call himself, a Ghostbuster.

My daddy didn't hold me down

My daddy didn't hold me down, no, he never got me.

All the girls were got but no, not me.

I hear them whisper under dark circles of watery arches

And in the sleeve of leaves along the quay.

My daddy wasn't fast enough to catch me

My daddy stumbled over quite a lot

He didn't haw his breathe upon my cheekbone

His snorting nostrils didn't spit and snot.

I didn't smell the sweetness of the cider

Or look into his glaucomatous eyes

I didn't scream and kick to get him off me

I didn't drown the Shannon with my cries

Street people think that they can see right through me,

Narrow eyes from girls and sneers from boys

They rail against the inside of my insides

But everything they heard is all just lies.

Caroline Coyle.

The Precious Present

By

Bernie Doyle

The precious present it's called. By present I mean the *now*. The *here*. As precious as a rare diamond you might say. But you can live without a rare diamond, can't you? So what way does the rare diamond make your life better? If you sell it you make a lot of money. Is money the answer to your feelings of worthlessness? As the song says: *money can't buy me love*. Ok you would have the money, to get you everything you want or need, freedom to travel and live in fabulous houses and places. You could have all the conditions required to satisfy anybody.

But.

You have to lie down with yourself at the end of the day. Whether or not the bed is full of desirable bodies is of no consequence. Because you are simply a slave to your attachments. But the precious present gives you the freedoms to see what's around you and experience all your feelings *without* having strings on it. What does that mean? It means when you don't have all your things around you, you suffer. This is called an *attachment*. And the lack of it causes you to suffer. You think having these attachments anchor you. But in fact they make you feel very insecure. When this starts to unravel and a situation arises in our lives that we haven't expected or prepared an attachment for we panic Most people at this point head off to the doctor for a quick fix. Imagine a ship on the high seas. When the storm comes the ship is knocked about. If it was attached to the harbour wall it would be pulled apart. This is what happens with all our attachments: they pull us apart. And we have a breakdown or worse: we create an illness and die.

Attachments are not just the obvious ones of alcohol, drugs, food, exercise, sex. You could be attached to always being right. A clean house, a glass of milk before bed. One is as bad as the other. The glass of milk is not the problem if you want it. It's the need that makes it different. You could have a need to be liked, or a need of people's approval. And there are loads more subtle ones. Again, think of yourself as the ship on the sea. If you have all these attachments you won't be able to sail the seven seas unimpeded. But to become aware of all these attachments is to know they are there in the first place.

Let's return to having that rare diamond. What does it add to you? I'm not saying you can't have all the goodies life has to offer, but it will be all the sweeter if you are coming from a place of appreciation. Of respect for the precious present. Perhaps, the error is comparing the precious present to a diamond in the first place. That's putting a limit on it. As the diamond is finite that's a mighty big difference. Even if the rock is the size of the Rockefeller centre, it couldn't possibly compare to the infinite value of the precious present.

So what *is* the precious present? Well, the official explanation is a moment by moment awareness. Does life become very simple when one is living in the present? And to achieve that do we have to go to a Buddhist retreat and contemplate life sitting under a tree at the foot of the Himalayan

Mountains? Is it only possible without the doings of ordinary life to distract us? Wouldn't that be so easy?

So how can we bring mindfulness into everyday life? Well I believe if we spend just five minutes each day and reflect on how we feel, this will help enormously. As we are vibrational beings we attract everything into our lives. So basically we create our own lives.

"Oh! No, it can't be that simple!" I hear you shout. It's so much easier to blame someone else for the negative effects of your attachments. Well, it's basically not taking responsibility *for you*. This might sound as if I'm flippant about this topic but stop for a moment and just ask yourself: How do I feel?

That is your guidance system and the clue is in the name. Does it do you any good feeling angry or resentful? No. It's "…negative vibes baby…." as Donald Sutherland says in *The Dirty Dozen,* and it's harming you.

Believe me, I've looked at this from all sides. Fear is the predominant emotion that stops people from becoming who they really are - their *authentic self* if you like. Actually there are only two emotions: Fear and Love. And every other emotion is a derivative of these. They are like the power grid of feelings.. To connect to the power grid you must use the precious present. I've heard it compared to a toaster. You being the toaster and the plug being the connection to the inner energy or power grid. The toaster won't work without plugging it in. Without focusing on the precious present.

Back to the wonderful question: How do I feel? You feel angry? Ok how does that connect you to the precious present? It's an energy that is in you but the important difference is that it's not *of you*. You are a spiritual being, having a human experience, so by knowing how you feel, you are connecting to that energy and then you can release it. You can't release it if you don't know it's there in the first place. You must recognise it and let it go. The official explanation of mindfulness is paying attention, in the now, without judgement. If you justify the anger you only increase the negative energy and attract more of the same. So you just notice the anger, feel it and release it. By justifying, you remain in negative juice. It stops you connecting to the divine energy.

I will finish with the analogy of a beautiful river. Sometimes the river gets clogged up with rubbish. Usually there is one big block (like a log) in the bank of the river. So before long all the rubbish catches on the log and the river, which was brimming with life, becomes choked off. The water becomes stagnant. All plant life in the river dies and all insects and animals that used the river no longer come here. Can the river recover? Oh yes, definitely! By removing the debris, one piece at a time, the river will recover in a very short time.

So how do you feel? The answer to that is removing negative energy (like the debris) one piece at a time.

The Devil's Pirouette

By

Jennifer McCarthy

The anticipation of that familiar burn had been nipping at my heels all day. Swirling the golden liquid around the crystal tumbler. I marvelled how something so unobtrusive could be both one's best friend and mortal enemy.

Over the glass rim I caught sight of the delicate ballet slippers hanging mockingly from the coat rail. I suppose I'd ruined them, just as I ruined everything. In my inebriated state I'd thought the idea amusing. While awaiting her return from one of Victor's extensive training sessions, I might have tried on those silken pumps; and perhaps one or two of her leotards for good measure. There was still a crack in the glass cabinet; courtesy of my ennui. My attempt at one of her fancy jumps had resulted in my tripping on the table leg and hurtling into the cabinet. She'd left me there that night; unconscious on the sitting room floor.

How long had it been since her departure? Two months? Three? This was the big one; the Titanic of chances, minus the iceberg of course—unless you added me into the equation. The analogy brought another image to mind; smiling, I pictured Victor trapped on one of those inflatable lifeboats; sailing away upon a never-ending ocean; a never-ending, shark infested ocean, with no drinking water—and the song yellow submarine on repeat.

Chasing the memories with the remaining whiskey, I reached down the side of the recliner to grasp the bottle by its neck; pouring heavily into the glass.

When next I looked up my gaze gravitated toward the mantle; where our wedding photo stood. How beautiful she had been, an angel come to walk the earth, mixing amongst us mere mortals for a day. A mistake; for she'd been seduced to the dark side by a demon in disguise—I was the phantom hidden in the opera house; preying on the innocent. Christ, I recalled our first dance; she'd allowed me lead—me; rhythm lacking, two left feet me, and she a dancer. She'd almost tripped in that spectacular lace dress. Resourcefully she'd used my waistcoat for leverage, the force of it ripping the stitching, causing the buttons to pop off; one determined button had even hit Aunt Clara in the eye; granted she was an irritating busybody. Still, another woman might have crumpled beneath the embarrassment—she'd laughed; a full, heart-warming laugh.

I remembered the first time I heard that sound, a siren's call that lit up the entire bar. I'd never really stood a chance, lost the moment my gaze caught sight of her. That gloriously lithe form; accentuated by the black fitted pants and slim fitted blazer she wore. Her shoulder length golden hair tumbling about her heart shaped face in soft waves. The way she'd moved; it had been grace personified. I'd been a besotted fool from day one.

Those days were long since passed. She was, at this very moment, the Prima Ballerina (Arora) in Tchaikovsky's Sleeping Beauty, and *the Russian* AKA Victor was her prince. But of course, he was the King to her Queen; with his dark looks and alluring accent. It was a love story in the making; maybe they could base a new ballet on it. I could even play the bad mouthed, whiskey drinking, covetous sorcerer—a definite sell hit; who wouldn't pay to see that?

Drinking deeply, I shuddered. I was the definition of cowardice; drowning in my own shame and self-loathing. What was preventing my seeing her? Perhaps fear of what I might find; could I salvage the remnants of this broken relationship—was there even a relationship to salvage? The arguments; the insults. I'd gone too far this time, said too many hurtful things. Lashing out at her because I'd felt so inadequate, so utterly lacking, so irrelevant. How was I to compare to *the Russian?* I didn't fit into that world—had I ever? I'd always been in awe that she'd chosen me—picked me.

Children; how she'd longed for them; prayed for them—but years of bodily abuse, of starvation had damaged her chances in the end. That devastation near broke us; but somehow, by some miracle we'd survived the heartache. She was so very strong; never sinking into the quicksand sorrow, no matter how hard it tried to pull her under. Shame filled me as I recalled my parting words—they ricocheted off the walls in silent rebuke. Even this poison wasn't diluting the memory; it had been engrained into my mind like an axe to wood; both painful and scarring. *"Maybe Victor's swimmers might be strong enough to keep a baby in that body of yours?"*

Downing a lengthy swig of the bottle I pushed back at the dark memory. No longer would I remember those vivid emerald eyes glinting with uninhibited humour, the echoes of her achingly beautiful laughter forever lost in the sands of time. All that remained was the grief those words triggered, her broken heart reflected in her gaze, staring dazedly at me as though I were a stranger. Never had I thought I'd be the one to cause such pain; to so callously open a barely healed wound. I'd finally done it—thrown the last stone; shattering the last shard of our relationship into irreparable pieces.

The bottle slid from my grasp and I allowed it fall—the contents spilling over the oak flooring. The motion had Odette, my Bichon Frise, tottering up to lick the residue. I laughed hollowly as her adorable nose scrunched up in distaste. Stepping away from the offending substance she leapt up on to the extended recliner. Placing two paws on my chest to lick my nose.

'Is there hope for me?'

Emitting a high pitched yelp she licked the wetness from my eyes; her attempt at soothing my battered soul.

'Not everyone's as forgiving.' I whispered

Rubbing Odette's soft pelt, I mulled over it all. Without Rose here the house felt so empty, so damned cold. I'd always known I didn't deserve her; but then again hadn't I always been a glutton for punishment. Grabbing the half empty bottle; I strode to the sink and poured; a symbolic gesture—but still; a start. As I watched the golden liquid swirl down the plug hole—I couldn't help but wonder—was it symbolic or was it prophetic?

****

Raising my hand, I positioned myself and bowed to the applauding audience. Once more the ballet was at its nightly close; and once more I was left feeling oddly forlorn. Accepting the usual bouquet's, I was steered backward by Victor's steady hand beyond the cascading curtain.

Russia hadn't been an easy feat—but then again anything worthwhile never was. Unfortunately my success had not been widely celebrated. My background was not of the elite and several of the chorus resented me for it. Regrettably it was the way of our world; everyone desired the spotlight---the competition fierce. I knew first-hand how difficult it was to rise to the top. I just wished when I looked into their eyes disdain wasn't staring back.

Thankfully Victor had been a great support; at first there may have been an expectancy behind his interest; and perhaps I'd been tempted—after all, I was all alone here; how easy it would have been to fall into his arms; to allow his protective nature shield me; to bask in a warmth I so often missed, but he was not for me. Victor deserved someone who could wholly be his.

One of the ballerinas broke away from the chorus and sidled up next to Victor. He rested his hand gently upon the small of her back; a gesture as tender as it was possessive.

'Would you like to join us for a nightcap?'

I dared a look at the red-haired Ballerina; who's name I thought was Irena. She did not appear keen.

'Another night perhaps?' I replied, feigning a yawn.

He nodded. Even with the beautiful Irena on his arm; I recognised the hint of regret in his dark gaze—guilt plagued me for any pain I might cause this man. Why couldn't Victor be the one taking up residence in my heart; why couldn't I love the safe, stable male before me?

Breaking away from the remaining dancers, I made my way backstage; toward my dressing room. As always memories slammed into my mind like powerful waves against a cliffside. Happy memories now tinged with inexorable sadness for what we'd become. He would never be what one would call conventionally handsome; but there had been a masculine ruggedness about him I'd found baldly attractive. From the start his hesitant approach to that nervous demeanour, had been nothing short of endearing. He had lacked the practised charm, the skilled flattery I'd been accustomed to. But even back then I'd known those shallow compliments would dwindle with time. He had been a breath of fresh-air, there had been something so raw in those midnight blue eyes. A hidden cynicism I'd recognised—a brokenness my inner demons had instantly reached for.

Spotting two young ballerina's depositing the audience's flowers at my dressing room's threshold, I paused—allowing them complete their task before entering my rooms. Melancholy pierced my heart at the sight. How I'd longed for children; ached to have five little fingers reach for mine; but it was not to be; my arms were destined to remain empty. Dancing was my life. In truth to get here I'd sacrificed so much—too much really.

Seated before the Hollywood style mirror; I stared at the reflection within. The stark loneliness in those emerald eyes was startlingly obvious; averting my gaze I peered down at my phone.

No Messages.

For the last four weeks a text had appeared each night; reading the same words. *Good Luck, Briar Rose.*

It was a private endearment only my estranged husband knew of—*Briar Rose* had been Disney's name for the lost Princess Arora—right now it was quite fitting.

With the lack of a message came a sizeable amount of anxiety. What if something terrible happened to him; how could I live on knowing that this had been it? I might miss the man he was, so fiercely it was crushing; but I did not wish him ill.

My chest constricted as my gaze flicked to the table where the vases of single roses stood. In line with the timing of the text messages, a card containing two words accompanied a red rose each evening. At first I hadn't understood. But once pinning the cards to the wall; the words of a familiar song came to light; a childhood favourite—Walt Disney's Sleeping Beauty 'Once upon a Dream'; where Prince Charming and Arora meet for the first time. Standing upright I strode toward the cards; my eyes stinging as I read the words aloud.

I know you,
I walked with you once upon a dream
I know you,
The gleam in your eyes is so familiar a gleam
Yet I know it's true
That visions are seldom all they seem
But if I know you
I know what you'll do
You'll love me at once, the way you did once upon----

The last words echoed unspoken in the air about me. Lifting my hand to my eyes; I swept the tears from my cheeks.

'*A dream…*' a deep baritone whispered

I whirled to find my dressing room door ajar. Beneath the doorframe knelt a dashing man in a tuxedo; holding a rose in his right hand; his left resting flat upon his chest. I couldn't speak; all I could do was stare into those clear, intelligent blue eyes—free of the red rimmed inebriation, free of the accusatory stare, free of the chains.

'I know I don't deserve it, my behaviour inexcusable. But if I could have but one thing in this entire world; one wish granted—I would beg for your forgiveness'

Tears fell freely as I recognised the genuine sincerity in his gaze. This was he; the man I remembered—not to sound too cliché; but the man I'd dreamt would return to me one day. He might have a ways to go; but my heart urged my head to let him back in. He would never be the Prince charming of children's fairytales; but seeing him kneeling there—laid bare and exposed I realised he would always be the Prince of my story.

'Philip?' I whispered past the lump in my throat

With one fell swoop I was engulfed in his embrace; and for the first time in months I was home.

Home

by

By Olivia Caffrey

Vida woke up confused again. For some time now her days were the same. And if not the same, they were devoid of an anchor to place the day, the time. Her days had lost all their structure.

Vida was never a very structured person, if she was to be completely honest with herself. When her children were small their house was chaotic. Perhaps *busy* was a better way to put it. She was so busy with working and getting the children out with a good breakfast, and in bed at a reasonable time, and tomorrow's lunches packed.

And now she couldn't find her glasses on the bedside table. She stepped gingerly out of the bed and groped around the little room to find them. It was handier sleeping in the small room now that the house was empty. It was warmer and less tidying was required. She would have been quite happy to just live in that little room if she could put some cooking things in there. She could even sit on her bed and fry an egg at the same time. Imagine that! Have it all set up so everything was on hand. A few pots and pans, a two ring cooker on a stool and some dishes conveniently placed. Like camping. She was quite the inventor. She often thought of handy little things to make her life easier domestically. Time saving ideas; now that she had a lot of time to think of them. Her daughter would cry out in horror when she mentioned some of her ideas so she rarely mentioned them and, mostly for that reason, they weren't executed either.

Recently, the children had organised and paid for a lady to come in and do the vacuuming and dusting but mostly she would come in and make a cup of tea and chat to Vida about her own children. Vida thought all six of them were doing law at Trinity but she wasn't sure. Sometimes she found it hard to concentrate when the woman spoke and would find herself staring at the shapes she made with her mouth, the tight *'o's*, the wide *'e's* and the long *'auuus'*. The woman's face getting smaller and her lips getting bigger, imagining just vowels streaming out randomly like bubbles from her mouth, floating in the air, lingering and pop! Giving Vida a little jolt. And then the woman started to speak more slowly for some reason and started using 'we' when she actually meant Vida herself and not the two of them. So Vida explained to the lady, one day, that she was fine because her daughter would be coming back home permanently, so she wouldn't be needing her services anymore. She felt a little bad lying but really, she could make her own tea for that price!

Vida finally found her glasses under the pillow beside her where they had slipped away as she had read herself to sleep. She'd had to unmake and remake the bed to find them. But now her day was finally starting.

Later that day, in another part of the world, Audrey's whole room was filled with sunlight as she had forgotten to close the curtains the night before. Her face was warm as she woke. As a little girl she often kept the curtains open in her room for the same effect. The weather didn't always keep it's promise and often her eyes opened to the streaks of rain creeping down the old cast iron framed windows, the rust peeling off in places on the frames, some of the little square panes cracked. She still liked the look of the green and the white and the grey outside blending in front of her sleepy eyes, as she lay there tiny, in a huge pillowy warm bed made with love, like a nest for a little chick.

This morning she leaped out of bed and stood to look at the vista in front of her. This everyday vista! She said to herself. She felt the same delight she had felt that morning, years ago, touching down for the first time: the weight of potential taking her breath away. This beauty always worked its magic even when things were not quite right. Every day, the Lilac in the garden and the lines of palms, black in the distance, the dawn behind them, created that slow dreamy haze of a Californian sunrise. She was content in this world. Although this morning another feeling grabbed her by the throat so suddenly she inhaled as if she had had a fright. Sadness tinged the edges of this picture, a feeling of panic even; the feeling in a dream when you are reaching for something and it is disappearing, or you are disappearing. She felt dizzy as she walked down stairs for coffee, the coffee helped. She was tired after the long shoot.

By noon everything was in full swing. The band was making quite a racket by the pool and Audrey was starting to regret the music she had chosen for the party. She thought *upbeat* would be perfect but didn't consider how loud the chatting and the splashing and the clinking of the caterers would be. She was exhausted, that was why. But everyone had turned up and seemed to be having a good time and soon she was laughing and sipping champagne and finally beginning to relax. She loved to throw parties. She loved watching people she liked or loved tentatively, or extravagantly, arriving at her door and how everyone somehow matched and fitted in the oddest ways; the alchemy of a group of people with different expectations but in silent agreement that you had to try your best.

Her mother has also been a great entertainer. She loved people. She was tall and she looked like a movie star. She lit up inside when she had guests and she would flutter around so graciously in her beautiful sitting room. Audrey thought it was beautiful. The sitting room was small, but had a large window facing the garden. On the walls hung many paintings collected by their parents from remote parts of the world, some so brightly coloured like a children's book that she and her brother would imagine stepping right into them and swimming in their warm aqua marine seas and basking in their orange beaming sunlight. There were also framed photographs taken by her mother, many of them of their father as a young man. In one of the children's favourites, he looked tanned and healthy and was laughing with love into the camera, into their mother's eyes. He had a halo of rainbow mist around him from the rushing water of the waterfall behind. The sun would set in that sitting room and turn everything golden, even on the colder days.

Suddenly she noticed a familiar looking parcel poking out amongst the presents that had been left on the trestle table near the garden doors. Her mother's present to her for her birthday: always on time, always wrapped in the same beautiful wrapping paper. Audrey opened the box carefully and inside was nestled a soft, pure white cashmere scarf, her mother's, from a long time go, perfect as if it had been bought yesterday. A precious thing, an untouchable thing Audrey had admired from when she was a little girl. She gently lifted it to her face and it smelt of roses and jasmine like the special clothes of her childhood, clothes that had been washed by hand with love by her mother.

Audrey thought back on her fifth birthday. Her mother had bought her a little pink coat with a fluffy white collar. She loved that coat so much and wore it everyday. She kept trying to wear it even when the sleeves were too short and the waistband was riding up and she couldn't really do up the buttons. It still looked like new but Audrey had grown. Her mother would smile at her when she would appear in the hall wearing it before one of their little adventures and would wordlessly bend down to help her to take it off and help her into her bigger coat. Her mother smelt of flowers and apples and warmth. Audrey never protested. It was really uncomfortable. But she always hoped each time when she took it out of the wardrobe it would fit! One day she took it out and handed it to her mother who wrapped it up, put it in a box, and gave it to a neighbour's child.

Audrey started to cry. It wasn't noticeable to anyone else. But she slipped away from the poolside where the party was and sat by herself in her white, bright empty sitting room. She sat in an oversized chair that was facing the sea and the muslin curtains were gently blowing like waves on the ocean, or like washing from her childhood. Nobody could see her if they walked in, she was so small in that chair. Her heart was breaking over the memory of this damn coat, and the softness of her mother's scarf against her skin and it all felt like home.

'Today is her birthday.' Vida told Mary in the post office (or was it Margaret?). 'So if I posted it on Tuesday it would definitely be there by today?'

'Yes, Vida, it would be there by yesterday. Unless something happened.'

'What could have happened?'

'Vida, nothing could have happened. I told you yesterday.'

The key was getting stuck in the door again and Vida was sweating as she struggled with her shopping and her gloves and her sleeves and the phone ringing mercilessly at the other side of the locked door. As she clicked the door behind her she stood in the hall in the silence that hurt her ears after the ringing had stopped.

The kitchen was nearly completely dark and she thought she should remember to put the light on before she leaves on days like this even though it is expensive. She always felt like she was holding her breath till summer came.

Ringing again! Vida had accidentally plugged out the answering machine her daughter had given her months ago when she was home for a visit, and couldn't figure out how to set it up again.

'Mum! Hello! Got you!'

'Audrey! Is that you?'

'Mum, It's me.'

'Happy Birthday you!'

'Happy Birthday me!'

And Vida sat on the upright chair beside the telephone table still wearing her coat and one glove and her eyes glistened as she told the story of when Audrey came into this world, as she did every year. 'And it was the coldest day of the year and you had no hair at all and I whispered so quietly, warm in your ear….my little baby, my lovely little baby, my little one….'

The Gathering

By

Gina Dunne

The dreaded day had arrived for the gathering, and the last minute arrangements were being finalised. An upmarket restaurant by the name of Theodore's had been selected by my sister Sheila, who presided over every detail with military precision.

This was the eve of my father's wedding to Celine, a renowned artist and flamboyant character, the total opposite to my late mother. Sheila had flown over 5000 miles from the Bahamas where she lived with Gareth - her partner of ten years. They had no children, though Sheila desired some, and often, after a few drinks, she became weepy and melancholy about her inability to conceive. She had always been an A+ student, college graduate of law (though never practiced) and was now a fashionable interior designer. A slight irony there as Sheila had always played it safe with colour, alcohol, boyfriends. Never stepping out of line and always maintaining the status quo. She was totally unlike me, the younger one, the total opposite. Continents apart in both looks, personality, taste in boyfriends, sex before marriage, drugs and rock & roll. You get the picture.

By the way, my name is Melody. Well not really but it's what I call myself now amongst my close friends and family members. My birth name is the Irish for Mary, *Maire,* with a fada. Very important as my mother supposedly summoned the registrar of Birth & Deaths to her bedside and chastised his inability to spell my name correctly. She was a formidable woman and one you should not have taken on lightly. Unfortunately, I didn't get to know her as she had passed before my first birthday.

So here we all were, seated like the Ewing family in Dallas, all trying to act normal while drinking copious amounts of alcohol to blur out the awareness of just being together. Seated at the top of the table was dad and his bride-to-be Celine. She was an established artist who had survived two marriages but the respective husbands had not and so my dad had become number three. My dad's name was Hugh and he had worked for over forty years as an accountant with the Brigs Waterman Group and retired just three years ago with the standard mantle clock and a modest pension. He and Celine had met on the Queen Mary 2 as it set sail from Southampton to New York. By the time it had reached New York six days later, the deed was done and now here we all sat wondering how long this would last, and who would get out alive.

Sheila sat on Gareth's right, monitoring his drinking, and occasionally giving him dagger looks as he directed his gaze in my direction. The fact that I opted to wear a jumpsuit with a plunging neckline didn't really help. But my logic was: *If you got it flaunt it. A*nd after spending 20k I needed to get value for money.

Gareth, ever the attention seeker, who liked the sound of his own voice, was now raising his glass to toast the happy couple. He was an obnoxious, overbearing overweight, middle-aged man, who was always afraid of being ignored. Something perhaps stemming from his boarding days and absent parents who lived in Geneva for tax purposes and throw money at him rather than affection. Perhaps it's no wonder he became an alcoholic and now he was knocking back the bourbon at a rate of knots. Sheila was trying desperately to conceal her anguish but her narrowed jawline and pinched up mouth gave the game away.

"To the happy couple hip hip hooray!!" Shouted Gareth.

As we took our seats, I looked across at Fr. Matthew. A fine specimen of a man. Early forties, six foot tall, with dark wavy hair, brown eyes and an orthodontic smile of gleaming teeth. He spoke with a slight English accent. I later found out he was born to English parents in North London, educated at the prestigious Glenstal Abbey in Murroe Co. Limerick and followed a career in Pharmaceuticals in both London and North Carolina, before he got the call from God.

As the dinner progressed and polite conversation ensued, I politely excused myself and headed outside for a much needed cigarette. The cool evening air was a refreshing welcome from the stifled atmosphere inside. As I pulled on the last drag, I felt a presence behind me. I turned around Fr. Matthew was standing there somewhat sheepishly watching me.

'Sorry,' he said. 'I didn't mean to sneak up on you.'

'Oh, don't worry. You need a break too I see?'

'Something like that. Would you mind if I had one?'

'One what? Oh, sorry you mean a cigarette? Sure help yourself. I didn't take you as a smoker.'

'Well, I'm not really. Gave them up when I joined, but I still long for one when I get the smell.'

We both stood there, our backs to the wall and savoured the nicotine release into the blood stream. It bonded us, and at that moment I saw myself as Mary Magdalene the temptress.

When I arrived back to the party Celine was talking about her trip to Florence and her visit to the Academia Gallery to view Michelangelo's statue of David.

'A masterpiece of Renaissance sculpture darlings.'

Dad said nothing and looked somewhat dejected and uncomfortable in his formal suit.

Dessert had arrived, including a large Pavlova cake in the shape of a heart, dotted with heart shaped strawberries all around the rim. I thought of some poor misfortunate on less than minimum wage having to slog for hours cutting these strawberries into hearts so that onlookers like us could ooh and aah at its arrival.

'Where's Gareth?' Asked Sheila suddenly.

'Must be gone to the loo,' I said. 'Come on, let's all eat some of that cake.'

But when I looked around I saw Gareth propped up at the bar, whispering sweet nothings into the ear of a twenty something blonde. He was holding a whiskey glass in his hand with the last dredges of bourbon evident. He was smiling widely and laughing at something the young girl said.

As Celine cut the cake into equal portions, and placed each slice carefully onto individual side plates, Sheila said she would go look for Gareth, she didn't want him missing out, and after all Pavlova was his favourite.

And that's when she looked around and saw him. And what he was up to. She got up and walked swiftly away from the table. I excused myself and quickly followed her. She walked straight to the bar, with me in hot pursuit. Gareth was too busy still enjoying the attention of this young twenty something. Sheila marched up to the counter like she was on marching parade duty, turned Gareth's chair around and, without uttering a single syllable, punched him right on the nose!

Blood spattered everywhere and the whiskey glass shot up into the air and then came crashing down, exploding into a hundred pieces. Gareth stood, somewhat unbalanced and still in shock and landed a punch so hard that Sheila was knocked backwards! I took the brunt of her weight as we both fell back, Sheila now lying directly on top of me. I closed my eyes, before impact and now lay there very still, hoping this was just a bad *bad* dream, but as I opened my eyes several other pairs were staring down at us.

At this point Gareth had been restrained by the duty manager and the twenty something blonde had run off and now a group of about fifteen people stood gaping down at us lying horizontally on top of each other.

As Sheila was helped up, somebody handed her a large linen napkin to hold to her nose. She was still bleeding profusely and the top of her cerise pink dress was now a darker shade of ruby. I got to my feet adjusting my jump suit so that my cleavage wasn't on public display, but nobody seemed interested as I stood up, pulling at my top. It was then I noticed Fr. Matthew standing at the entrance of the bar. As he approached, he had a worried look in his eyes.

'Your dad has collapsed, you need to come.'

We both ran back to the restaurant. Celine was on her knees, tears streaming down her face as she was holding dad's hand and rubbing his fingers, willing him to open his eyes. The paramedics had arrived, and preceded to clear the area, and put dad into the recovery position, before starting chest compressions. They worked solidly for fifteen minutes but it made no difference.

Time of death 10.42pm.

Gareth had arrived back just as Fr Matthew was administering the last rites. He was somewhat flustered and embarrassed but as the drama played out in front of him he looked visibly weak and shocked at what he was witnessing.

Dad's body was removed to the local morgue that night.

Two days later we gathered again, standing at the graveside like an awkward group of strangers. Nobody making eye contact and listening to the faint sobs of Celine as she held a single rose, waiting to be cued by Fr. Matthew to release it.

The drive back to the house was very much a silent affair, each of us caught up in the moment of our own grief. When we arrived, the caterers were already in situ, placing large trays of canapés and bite size sandwiches onto tables and ladling out large pots of thick soup from the stove. Neighbours, friends, and past work colleagues of dads were all there, mixed in with Celine's artistic and well heeled circle. It truly was a motley gathering of the rich and not so famous.

I sat back in dad's old armchair remembering the many times we shared, as a little girl sitting on his knee, to an adolescent crying on his shoulder because my whole world had fallen apart. Our bond could not be broken, and he was my best pal, confidant and avid supporter.

People started to move away, shaking hands, sympathising once again, giving words of encouragement, time heals etc....

When the last of the funeral party had left, and the caterers had loaded up the van, Celine asked us to join her.

We all sat down together in the little sitting room at the front of the house. The dying embers of the fire glowing faintly, the room warm and familiar. Celine came in and closed the door. In her hand she held a bottle of Jameson whiskey and five glasses. Placing them on the small table she opened the whiskey and poured a generous measure into four glasses, putting ginger ale into one. Handing a glass to each of us, with one remaining on the table, she picked up her drink and asked us to raise ours in remembering the man who we all had the pleasure of knowing.

Leaving Legacy

by

By *Sheila Mahon*

I sat in the waiting area of the old Georgian house and felt uneasy. Heart pounding, palms sweaty.

'It'll be grand,' smiled Michael beside me.

Just then the door opened, a portly man stood at the doorframe. No eye contact, through his low rimmed specs.

'Theresa Byrne?' He asked - as if there was a lengthy queue.

'Yes'.

'Follow me'.

His name was Mr. Fitzgerald and he was a solicitor. We retreated to his office and it was no surprise to see Brigid Dunne, Robert's niece, sitting with her husband. She didn't look happy, though.

Fitzgerald broke the silence. 'Take a seat. Now, before we begin, I only require the ladies be present. However, if nobody objects, your husbands can stay.' Everyone nodded in agreement. The husbands stayed.

'Let's begin, then.' Continued Fitzgerald. 'Do you know why you are here today?' He looked straight at me.

'No, I just received a call to say I had to attend in relation to the legal matters of Mr. Robert Burns.'

'Yes, you knew him well I take it?'

'Well, he was a neighbour. My husband purchased our site, with a bit of land, from him.'

'I wouldn't call twenty acres *a bit*!' Brigid interjected. I was taken aback by her tone. This wasn't like her. She was normally so friendly.

'You're not related then?' Asked the solicitor.

'*I'm* his only living relative.' Said Brigid, her annoyance at our presence beginning to show.

'No, no relation, just neighbours.' I said, and glanced at Michael.

'Okay, interesting. Well I suppose I'll get straight to it.' Continued Fitzgerald.

The next twenty minutes passed in a blur. While I could hear Mr. Fitzgerald's voice, the words were not making sense. My brain couldn't register. My throat felt dry. The only thing I remembered was when Michael spoke.

'Let me get this straight? Robert has left my wife *all* of his worldly possessions?'

'No, not all. He left his niece some family heirlooms.'

'This is not right, what did you do?' Shrieked Brigid. 'How did you convince him to change his will?'

'I…I didn't know anything about this! I just checked in on him, I…'

'Took advantage of an ageing man? Everyone knew he had dementia in the end. This is elder abuse. Well this isn't the end of this - I want to contest the Will!'

'I should point out that this Will was made eight years ago and it's the only Will Mr. Burns has on record.' Said Mr. Fitzgerald.

'I think we should all calm down.' Said Michael. 'Did Mr. Burns explain *why*? Did he leave a letter?'

'No explanation. No letter. He came to my office and made the will with witnesses and left.'

'You BITCH!' Said Brigid. 'I'll not let you get away with this.'

'Brigid, I don't know why this has happened but I can assure you: It's as much of a shock to me, as it is to you.'

With that, Brigid and her husband left, slamming the door on the way out. Mr. Fitzgerald tutted and began to talk again. I couldn't take it in. I was numb. Why would Robert Burns leave me his two hundred acre farm? I hardly knew him.

Michael was local and I, Theresa Higgins, was not. I was the only child of Kate Higgins, an unmarried mother that *wasn't* sent to the mother and baby home from our village of Ballycur. My mother had been proud and strong. She'd farmed with my grandfather and could do the work of any man. It was my grandfather that ran the priest. He always brought her to mass during her pregnancy and made her stand tall. He was a ferocious man that had fought the black and tans and saved half the village from ruin during the war.

My mam never married.

My father left before I was born.

Then mam died six years ago after a short illness.

I needed her, to talk to her, I missed her. Then I thought of Josie, her longest and closest friend.

I drove towards the cottage. It looked smaller. The same old Rosebush, wild and spread over the door. The little box hedges keeping her flowers safe from wildlife. It brought back childhood memories, picking apples, making jam, baking apple pies.

'Hello, Josie. It's only me!'

'Come in, Theresa, come in! Let me see you.'

We embraced, the kitchen smelt the same, turf mixed with pearl soap and flash powder.

'It's so good to see you. I knew you'd come. I heard all about it.'

'You heard *what?*'.

'The land. You were left a farm'.

'God, news travels fast.'

'I was delighted. You deserve every grain. Every blade of grass and every bale of hay'.

'What makes you say that, Josie?'

'What did Kate say?'

'Kate's gone, Josie. She died, remember?'

'Kate saw him at your wedding. Michael had invited him. Kate knew him straight away. She nearly fainted'.

'Saw who? Mam hadn't eaten that morning and felt a bit unwell'.

'Is that what she told you? Weak at the knees she was. She never thought she'd see him again.'

'Who Josie, who?!'

'The dead man. Burns….'

'Josie, are you saying….? Did my mother know Robert Burns?'

'She did! We *both* did. She swiped me eye in Ballycur hall. I was eyeing his brother Richard and she just smiled at him and that was it. I had no hope.'

'Mr. Burns had a brother? I never knew that'.

'Aye, it was a long time ago. He was a fine handsome man that went to America. He dressed in a fine suit and he wore *Old Spice*. You'd suffocate if you to had stand near him too long.'

'What was his name, Josie?'

'Richard. Richard Burns. He never returned. Few did in them days. 'She began to cry.

'Ah Josie, don't cry. It's okay.'

'No. It's not okay. What they did to your mother, poor Kate. Poor beautiful innocent Kate. It was a sin and they will rot in hell for it.'

'What do you mean?'

'That mother of his, that auld bitch. She wouldn't let them marry. They said special prayers for her evil deeds at her funeral.'

I got a fright when the door suddenly creaked open.

Her Carer came in.

'Hello Josie, how are you?' Asked The Carer.

Josie sobbed and as I handed her a tissue. She put a single finger to her lips to *shush me*. My questions would have to wait.

'I better go, sorry if I upset you.'

'You didn't upset me. You haven't been here long. You didn't even get tae!'

'I have to get the kids from school. I'll come again soon.'

Mam had never mentioned a Richard Burns or his family. Josie was forgetful but she seemed so sure. But Robert had never said that he knew my mother. I remembered my wedding day and how Mam was unwell and couldn't eat her food. And then I suddenly recalled how Michael was giving out that his neighbour Burns only came for the feed as he left straight after the wedding dinner.

About a week later, I had the keys of Robert's farm house and decided to go see if I could find something. A clue, anything to connect us. I opened the door and the smell of dampness and soot hit me.

There wasn't much furniture and I could see his old armchair battered and worn. I sat on the edge and looked around the old room, something caught my eye. It was an old news clipping hanging near the calendar. It was about a Richard Burns going to America. I couldn't help wonder:

Did he get my Mam pregnant and leave?

Was that what happened?

Was he my father?

Is that why Robert left it to me?

I walked around and found a room with floral wall paper. There were some old dark religious photos there - the ones with the eyes that followed you round the room.

As I opened the wardrobe doors I found dresses and coats hanging there, like a museum piece untouched by time. This was Mrs. Burn's room. I looked down. Her old dusty grey shoes at the bottom and then, through a fluke of sunlight, something caught my eye. It was dark mahogany. The same colour as the wardrobe.

I sat on the bed with the box in my hands and opened the lid. It had receipts and papers and a few bits of old jewellery. I pressed the side and the bottom came apart and a small diary fell out. My heart began to pound. I knew I was meant find this. I admired the beautiful hand writing in delicate curves, flowing across the page.

Nervously I began to read:

May 1968

I am worried about Robert and Richard. They work day and night and show no sign of courting. I want my boys to find good matches, the local girls are not suitable. They all come from small farms and just want our land. I will go to O'Dea's Tailors and get them new suits. It will help. Only the best for my boys. A good match will be the making of them.

August 1968

The boys went to a dance in the next parish, Ballycur. They were in their new suits. They met undesirable trollops. I nearly burnt the suits when I heard it. I didn't pay that kind of money for them to go picking up some local hussy whose father is after our land. My boys will marry well if it's the last thing I do.

November 1968

The boys aren't speaking. Their father had to separate them the other night. Richard had Robert by the throat and said he was going to kill him. Father is worried. He thinks it's over a girl. Robert has standards like his mother. Richard is more like his father. Too relaxed. I'll not have some Ballycur hussy causing havoc in my family.

February 1969

A Ballycur man arrived accusing Richard of getting his daughter pregnant. Saying he forced himself on her. I know my son and I know that's not true. These hussies will say anything to get our land. I had the gun and told him my son had nothing to do with his daughter and to never set foot near our farm again. He threatened to burn us out of it.

March 1969

Richard wants to marry the girl from Ballycur who is pregnant. He's saying it's his child. The shame of it! Father has suggested we let them go to America. I want my boys with me, not in a foreign land. When I told Richard he could not marry her he went crazy. He was like a mad man. He said he couldn't live under our roof. Richard frightened the life out of his little sister, Mary Beth, and as I write tonight she has fallen asleep sobbing. The boys have become so estranged that they won't even sit in the same room, when one enters the other leaves.

April 1969

I am broken. My heart is torn in two. Why God, did you forsake me? All I ever asked was for you to take care of my boys. Robert has barely spoken. He wants to tell that girl about Richard. And Mary Beth cries. She's missing him, so. Father said I am never to mention his name again under this roof. My poor boy, my Richard. We couldn't even give him a Christian burial. He was buried in the darkness of night - behind the graveyard walls.

I curse Fr. Conlon how could he?

I put down the diary. *What was I reading?* Richard died? The newspaper clipping said he went to America. I knew only one person who might be able to help me. I had to go and see Brigid.

Heart in my mouth, I knocked on the door.

'What do you want?'

'We need to talk, Brigid. I need to ask you about Richard.'

'Richard who? '.

'Your mother's brother: Richard'.

Brigid tried to shut the door.

I wedged my foot as she pressed hard to close it. 'I need to know about Richard and then I'll leave'.

'What about him? He went to America and they never heard from him.'

I handed her the diary: ''Ten minutes, please…?'

Brigid reluctantly asked me to come in.

We sat reading the pages.

After, I asked: 'Am I Richard's daughter?'

'I don't know!'

Brigid explained that her mother never discussed him. She said Richard was the adventurer, handsome and worldly. Robert was quietly heartbroken. The brothers were close, according to my mother.'

'The only people buried behind the graveyard wall were still born babies or suicides. Your grandmother was a proud woman. Look at the date, Brigid, on the newspaper clipping: **Friday, 31st April 1969.** After the row in March and the April entry…did they want to cover up the suicide? Stop the gossip, avoid the shame?'

'Maybe. I don't know. There is an old Jacobs tin that I took from Robert's room. I haven't opened it yet. Hold on, I'll get it'.

As the two women sat at the kitchen table that day, they unravelled the Burns family secret. Richard's death cert was in the box. He had died at his own hands on 29th March 1969. He had never gone to America and was buried in the village outside the graveyard wall.

They found an envelope in a small bible. The letter was written in May 1969

Dear Mother and Father,

I write this as I need you to understand and clear my conscience. I saw Kate first and danced with her. If her friend Josie hadn't introduced her to Richard, Kate would have been mine. I didn't mean to hurt her. I just wanted her to love me but she only had eyes for Richard. Kate never told Richard it was me that got her pregnant, that I forced myself on her. It was passionate rage, I wanted her to be mine, felt I deserved her. I told Richard that Kate was carrying my child and offered to marry her. But that night Richard left. He went to the barn with a broken heart. I didn't follow him. Please forgive me.

Your son always,

Robert.

About the Authors:

Janice Dobbie though originally from Co. Antrim settled in Athlone in 1976. She has been writing fiction on and off for many years plus a little poetry. In the past this has been published in Athlone's Writers Group publications. Janice is currently retired and can be contacted at saraijane@gmail.com

Olivia Caffrey lives in Athlone with her husband and children, having moved from London three years ago. This is her first creative writing course and first publication.

John McLoughlin is native to the parish of Rahan, close to Tullamore, Co. Offaly, where he still lives. His first foray into writing came with attendance at AIT's Creative Writing course in 2018. The short story is John's preferred writing form. John is contactable at johnmcloughlin63@gmail.com

Peggy Garvey grew up in Co Wexford. She enjoys writing short stories. She is a retired Primary Teacher who is interested in reading, psychology, history and gardening. She lives with her husband in Athlone. Email: peggygarvey@outlook.ie

Anne Marie Crehan was encouraged by a friend at work to join the very first Creative Writing Class at Athlone I.T. and has thoroughly enjoyed the experience. Originally from Co. Galway, Anne Marie lives in Keoghville outside Athlone with her husband Pat and they have three daughters. This is her first attempt at writing.

Bernie Doyle is from athlone. She teaches mindfulness and meditation in schools. This is her second publication. She also produced a CD and booklet on meditation. "Like every other fledgling writer, I believe there is a book in me." Contact: berniedoyle@live.ie

Sheila Mahon from Rosenallis Co Laois. She writes poems, local pieces and non-fiction stories She wrote her first story at age seven and has since been published in the local paper *The Leinster Express* and her poem was read at *The Remembrance Run* at the Phoenix Park last November.

Marva Fitzpatrick currently lives in Moate and works as a lecturer in the Department of Nursing and Health Sciences at the Institute of Technology, Athlone. She has been writing for approximately four years. This is her first publication. Mfitzpatrick22@outlook.com.

Chantalle Loughran originally hails from Sydney and now lives in Athlone. She took up writing fiction as a hobby while on maternity leave. You can contact her on: chantalleloughran@gmail.com

Jennifer McCarthy is a native of Tullamore town. From an early age she enjoyed the art of creative writing, specifically stories with a fantastical element. You can contact her: jenmccarthy1@live.ie

Gina Dunne is a Limerick Girl 20 plus years in the Midlands.
Did some writing during her college days, worked in many different careers from education to outplacement consultancy to now working on a contract basis with the HSE in Community Care. Would love to continue writing and hopefully one day be published.

David Whelan is a Carlow native. He enjoys writing primarily fiction. This is his first publication. He currently works in the pharmaceutical industry.

Joe Dowling is a native of Athlone. He has been writing magazine articles and poetry for a short while. His efforts have been published in the Irish Defence Magazine and the Limerick leader. He is retired and can be contacted at jmdowling50@hotmail.com.

Oliver J Higgins is a native of Doonis the Pigeons in the parish of Tang, County Westmeath. He currently lives in Williamstown, Mullingar, County Westmeath. He wrote his first poem while attending Tang school. Since then, he has written poetry for the students of Thomas Russell middle school in Milpitas California, Poetry in the Park Athlone, The Etb adult learning centre yearly journal Longford, and the Carrickedmond Annual Parish Newsletter and also had a piece printed in the Sunday Independent that was written for his late father Jack Higgins (also known as the Thatcher). He now writes almost every day. Mostly poetry and the odd short story and some Non-fiction. He can be contacted on *revilojsniggih2015@gmail.com*

David Flynn is from Athlone. He's been involved in different kinds of writing all of his life. Since he joined the course he has pushed his writing boundaries further, and is working on a number of different projects. David has made many friends on the course who have inspired him, and he believes that writing in some form or other will always be part of his life.

Aideen O'Hara is returning to her early love of writing, after a very long absence. She settled back in her home town of Roscommon before having a family. Email aideen.ohara@hse.ie

Raphael O'Brien from Rosemount Moate. In primary school he entered an All Ireland writing competition organised by CRC Clontarf and came Third in Ireland for his School. He began writing again this year when he started a Creative Writers Workshop organised by IWA Clontarf in conjunction with the Irish Writers Centre Dublin. He has attended both of Mick's courses since Sept 2018. He found then very enjoyable and Enlightening.

Caroline Coyle is a poet and performance artist. Founder of The Art of Possibilities Community Drama Group, she utilities the mediums of poetry, drama, music and art to engage the community. She has been a student of the writing class for two semesters as well as a Guest Speaker.

Editor: Mick Donnellan. Mick is from Mayo and currently lives in Athlone. He teaches the Creative Writing Class at the AIT under the Department of Life Long Learning. You can read more about Mick on www.mickdonnellan.com

Printed in Poland
by Amazon Fulfillment
Poland Sp. z o.o., Wrocław